"I have no idea what you just said, but the words sure sounded good rolling off your tongue."

"The language is irrelevant," Jenny answered coolly. "The point is you're blocking the door."

"I'm Richard Warren." He offered his hand.

After a brief hesitation, she accepted it, her initial reluctance bolstered by the unwelcome tingle that reverberated through her system. "Jenny Anderson."

"Have we met before?"

"No." Her tone was as succinct as the single-word response.

"Are you sure?" he pressed. "Because you really look familiar to me."

"I'm sure, and if that's all—"

"It's not," he said. "It turns out that I have the next few days free—and I was hoping that you might be willing to show a fellow American around."

"You might have the next few days free, Mr. Warren, but I don't."

"How about the nights?"

HER BEST-KEPT SECRET

BRENDA HARLEN

SPECIAL EDITION®

Published by Silhouette Books

America's Publisher of Contemporary Romance

Special thanks and acknowledgment are given to Brenda Harlen for her contribution to the FAMILY BUSINESS miniseries.

 SILHOUETTE BOOKS

ISBN 0-373-24756-7

HER BEST-KEPT SECRET

Visit Silhouette Books at www.eHarlequin.com

Printed in U.S.A.

Books by Brenda Harlen

Silhouette Special Edition

Once and Again #1714
Her Best-Kept Secret #1756

Silhouette Intimate Moments

McIver's Mission #1224
Some Kind of Hero #1246
Extreme Measures #1282
Bulletproof Hearts #1313
Dangerous Passions #1394

BRENDA HARLEN

grew up in a small town surrounded by books and imaginary friends. Although she always dreamed of being a writer, she chose to follow a more traditional career path first. After two years of practicing as an attorney (including an appearance in front of the Supreme Court of Canada), she gave up her "real" job to be a mom and to try her hand at writing books. Three years, five manuscripts and another baby later, she sold her first book—an RWA Golden Heart winner—to Silhouette.

Brenda lives in Southern Ontario with her real-life husband/hero, two heroes-in-training and two neurotic dogs. She is still surrounded by books ("too many books," according to her children) and imaginary friends, but she also enjoys communicating with "real" people. Readers can contact Brenda by e-mail at brendaharlen@yahoo.com or by snail mail c/o Silhouette Books, 233 Broadway, Suite 1001, New York, NY 10279.

This project came together with a lot of help
from various people and I'd like to thank:
Susan Litman, for inviting me to be part of the
FAMILY BUSINESS continuity;
the other fabulous authors of this series,
for answering all my questions and making
this project so much fun;
Jeff Mahoney, for information and insights
about working in the newspaper business;
Dave Ferguson, for stories and pictures
from his trip to Tokyo;
Bruce and Peggy Wallace, for sharing
their cottage so I can escape to my writing;
my mom, who watches the kids while I escape;
and especially my husband, Neill,
who loves me even when I'm under the pressure of
deadlines (because I know that isn't easy!)

Chapter One

Richard Warren waited outside the fourth floor board-room hoping like hell that the difficulties of the past twenty-four hours weren't an indication of things to come. He helped himself to a desperately needed cup of coffee and stood back, on the fringes of the crowd, searching for Morito Taka. It was by invitation of the CEO of TAKA Corporation that Richard was attending this meeting today.

As legal counsel for Hanson Media Group, his sole purpose was to observe and report back to his boss, Helen Hanson. Only after the proposed merger was approved by the majority of shareholders would Richard take an active role in negotiating the terms with TAKA's executive and its legal team. If all went according to schedule, everything would be finalized within the next few weeks and he could go back to his life in Chicago.

He hoped all went according to schedule. This merger was too important for anything to go wrong. In the six months since the death of George Hanson, his widow had done everything possible, if not more, to save the company from bankruptcy. And with almost no help from her husband's three children, who were too busy resenting Helen's position in the company to appreciate the sacrifices she'd made and the work she'd done.

But Richard forgot about his boss and everything else when he spotted the goddess across the room, all rational thought obliterated by three simple letters: W-O-W.

His gaze skimmed over her sling-back shoes, up endlessly long legs to the short, slim-fitting skirt and neatly tailored pin-striped shirt that hugged feminine curves, to the elegant knot of copper-colored hair at the back of her neck. She turned, giving him a glimpse of glossy peach lips, high cheekbones, and deep green eyes, and he felt as if all of the oxygen had been sucked out of the room.

It was attraction, immediate and intense. But it was also recognition, and that shook him more than the desire stirring in his blood. He was sure that he'd seen her before. And yet, he was equally certain she was a stranger.

Maybe jet lag was scrambling his brain—it was the only explanation for such an incongruous thought.

She poured herself a cup of coffee, glancing up as she brought the cup to her lips. Their eyes met across the room, just for a second, before her gaze slid away again.

Richard felt a stirring of desire and realized it had been quite some time since he'd wanted a woman. Somewhere over the past year, he'd simply lost interest in the pretenses and deceptions that were an integral part of the mating ritual.

But he was definitely interested now.

He turned toward her just as a voice spoke behind him. "Mr. Warren?"

Mentally cursing the interruption, Richard nevertheless put a smile on his face and turned. "Yes, I'm Richard Warren."

"I'm Yasushi Nishikawa." The young Japanese man bowed, offering a business card that he held in both of his hands.

Richard set his cup aside to accept the card, carefully reading the inscription before sliding it into the pocket of his jacket. Yet another helpful TAKA employee; yet another name to remember. He retrieved one of his own cards and presented it in the same manner.

"I have been given the honor of sitting with you to interpret the proceedings," Yasushi told him.

Richard nodded. *"Arigato."* Thank you.

The translator grinned. "You are learning our language."

"It's one of the few words I know," Richard admitted. He'd added good morning, excuse me and I don't understand—which he imagined he would be using frequently over the next few weeks—to his repertoire by studying his Japanese phrase book over his first cup of coffee that morning.

"It's a good start," Yasushi said. "I've also been asked to tell you that the commencement of negotiations has been delayed."

So much for keeping things on schedule.

"Mr. Tetsugoro was called out of town this morning on personal business. A death in the family," Yasushi explained. "He sends his apologies along with a promise to return by Monday morning."

While the man could hardly be blamed for a family emergency, Richard knew that would be little consolation to Helen with the future of Hanson Media at stake. He considered trying to call his boss now to advise her of this delay, but the meeting was scheduled to begin at eight o'clock and the sea of suits was already starting to flow toward the open doors of the conference room. The copper-haired goddess merged with the crowd that walked past.

Richard picked up his briefcase and followed Yasushi inside. Helen would have to wait.

He wasn't sure if it was lucky or not that his assigned companion selected a pair of chairs directly across the table from the woman who'd caught and held his attention.

"Jenny Anderson," Yasushi said softly, following the direction of his gaze. "She moved to Tokyo from New York about six months ago and is a society reporter for the Tokyo *Tribune,* TAKA's English language newspaper."

"Is it common for reporters to attend shareholder meetings?" he asked.

"No," Yasushi said. "But her parents are shareholders. She sometimes attends meetings on their behalf when they are out of the country."

A beautiful young reporter with jet-setting parents. The scant information didn't begin to answer all of the questions that came to mind.

He watched her riffle through a sheaf of papers she'd set on the table, and noted the absence of rings on her hands. He knew that wasn't conclusive evidence of anything, just as he knew that her marital status shouldn't be any of his concern. There was too much riding on this merger to allow his attention to be diverted, and the last thing he needed right now was the distraction of a woman.

Still, he found himself asking, "Is she married?"

Yasushi smiled. "No, but determinedly unavailable, much to the disappointment of every single man in this room."

Jenny hated these meetings, but she'd been unable to avoid this one as both of her parents were out of town and had left her with their proxies. When the final votes were taken and the meeting adjourned after a long and tedious three hours, she quickly slipped out of the room.

Unfortunately, she wasn't quick enough to avoid Kogetsu.

Cornered by the coffee pot, Jenny decided to pour herself another cup as she listened to his speech. Kogetsu was always trying to persuade or cajole or even bribe Jenny to visit his sister's art gallery in the hope that she would write it up for the society pages of the paper. She didn't object to giving some free publicity to a struggling entrepreneur, but she'd already written two articles about the gallery in the past four weeks. Lucky for Kogetsu, Jenny liked his sister, the gallery and usually the art she showcased.

She nodded her head in response to his enthusiastic call to support local up-and-coming artisans and glanced at her watch, hoping he would take the hint that she needed to be somewhere else soon. Of course, he did not, and she was forced to stand and listen another few minutes before she could interject to remind him that she wrote feature pieces, not advertising copy.

Somehow Kogetsu managed to look wounded by her remark, forcing Jenny to admit she'd already planned to cover the event—because it was an event and not because he'd asked her. Kogetsu didn't care about her reasons, of course, and she bit back a sigh as she turned away.

She'd taken only three steps toward the door when *he* stepped into her path.

He being a man she'd never seen before. At least, not before she'd caught him staring at her before the meeting. And several times during the endlessly long ordeal.

He was American—she'd known that immediately. It was more than just his impressive height and Western style of dress, it was the aura of success and self-confidence he wore as easily as the tailored suit jacket that stretched across his broad shoulders. She knew the type—she'd already fallen in love with and had had her heart broken by other men who fit the same mold. New York would be her first guess. Maybe Boston or Philadelphia. But definitely American and definitely trouble.

She spoke to him in Japanese, knowing he wouldn't understand the words and hoping he'd take the hint that she didn't want to talk to him.

His lips curved in an easy smile, but she wasn't in a mood to be charmed.

"I have no idea what you just said," he responded in English, "but the words sure sounded good rolling off your tongue."

"She said, 'Please, excuse me,'" Yasushi translated for him.

Jenny couldn't help but be amused by the deliberately loose interpretation of her words. "Actually what I said was, 'You're in my way.'"

The American's smile never wavered. "It sounded so much prettier in Japanese."

"The language is irrelevant," she said coolly. "The point is that you're blocking the door."

"I'm Richard Warren." He offered his hand.

After a brief hesitation, she accepted it, her initial reluctance bolstered by the unwelcome tingle that reverberated through her system. "Jenny Anderson."

"A pleasure to meet you, Jenny Anderson." He lowered his voice conspiratorially. "Is it safe to assume we won't need a translator for the next few minutes?"

"I don't have a few minutes." She realized he was still holding her hand and quickly tugged it from his grasp.

"Two minutes," he said, nodding to Yasushi, who discreetly stepped away.

She glanced at her watch, not bothering to hide her impatience. She had no inclination or interest in making conversation with any man whose simplest touch could affect her in such a way. Not any more. "Two minutes," she agreed.

He smiled again, clearly a man accustomed to getting his own way. "Have we met before?"

"No." Her tone was as succinct as the single word response.

"Are you sure?" he pressed. "Because you really look familiar to me."

"I'm sure, and if that's all—"

"It's not," he said.

She shifted the leather folio she carried from one hand to the other.

"It turns out I have the next few days free," he continued. "And I was hoping you might be willing to show a fellow American around."

"You might have the next few days free, Mr. Warren, but I don't."

"How about the nights?"

"Excuse me?" She shook her head, convinced she couldn't possibly have heard him correctly.

"It wasn't an indecent proposal," he said, then gave her another one of those heart-stopping smiles. "I was suggesting that you could show me the sights after you finish work."

"I don't think—"

Her refusal was interrupted by arrival of Shiguro Taka, making her wonder if she would ever get out of the building and back to her own job.

"Miss Anderson." He gave a slight bow before turning his attention to the American, bowing more deeply. "Mr. Warren. I wanted to apologize personally for the mix-up at the airport yesterday."

"Not a problem," Richard said.

"It was a poor reflection of Japanese hospitality. You must let us somehow make up to you the inconvenience."

Jenny managed a small step closer to the door before Richard shifted, again blocking her path.

"That really isn't necessary," he responded to Mr. Taka's offer.

"It is," Shiguro insisted. "Perhaps tickets to the Kabuki theater or sumo tournament."

"Well, I was hoping that someone might be able to show me around the city."

The other man nodded. "We have any number of employees who would be eager to take you on a tour of the sights."

"Actually," Richard said, "I was hoping that Ms. Anderson might be persuaded to fill that role."

"Of course," Shiguro said. "I can understand that you would enjoy the company of a fellow American, and an especially beautiful one at that."

He smiled in her direction, and Jenny got a sinking feeling in the pit of her stomach.

"I'm sorry, sir, but as much as I'd like to help—" it was

a lie, but one she had no compunction about uttering "—I don't have any time to spare over the next few days. I'm in the middle of an assignment for Lincoln Kelly and—"

"Mr. Kelly can reassign it," Shiguro said easily, already pulling his cell phone out of his pocket.

And he had the power to see that it was done, Jenny acknowledged bleakly. She might not work directly for Shiguro, but he was one of the key executives at TAKA and TAKA owned the newspaper.

Frustration churned inside her. She'd spent weeks on research-interviewing witnesses and corroborating facts—because she knew that this story would prove her skills as a journalist and open up new opportunities for her. If she lost this story, it could be months, maybe even longer, before another opportunity came along. More importantly, if she lost this story, she'd renege on a promise she'd made.

"It's an important story, sir—"

"Nothing is more important than showing our visitor proper Japanese hospitality," Shiguro countered.

Of course not—Japanese hospitality was legendary. And though she had no idea who Richard Warren was or why he was in Tokyo, it was obviously important to Mr. Taka to make a good impression on him.

As he started to dial the phone, the opportunity Jenny had waited too long for already slipped from her grasp.

She was furious.

Not that Richard could blame her, considering the way she'd been manipulated by Shiguro Taka and himself. The TAKA executive had steamrolled over her objections and coerced her into being his tour guide for the next couple of days, and Richard hadn't protested.

As he followed her hurried strides across the parking lot to the newspaper building next door, he was thinking he should regret his part in the whole arrangement. Should, but didn't. He was too intrigued by this woman and already looking forward to the opportunity to know her better.

She stormed past the reception desk and into what he guessed was the newsroom. She dropped her folio onto a desk and dropped into the chair behind it.

Richard stayed on the other side of the desk, a safe distance away. "You're angry."

"You're incredibly insightful." She picked up a pile of message slips and began sorting through them.

"Would it help if I said I was sorry?

She glanced up through narrowed eyes. "Are you?"

"Not really," he admitted.

"Then, no, it doesn't help." She crumpled up one of the messages and tossed it toward the garbage.

It missed.

Richard bent over to pick up the discarded scrap of paper and drop it into the metal can. "I've had a hellish two days," he told her. "My head is swimming with names I can't possibly remember, and when I saw you, I thought we might have something in common—two Americans in Tokyo."

"It sounds like the title of a bad movie."

Despite the derisive response, he noticed that she sounded more resigned than angry now.

"Is it really so horrible—a couple of days off to play tour guide?"

"Yes," she said through clenched teeth. "I don't want to play tour guide, I want to play reporter. That is, after all, why I went to college and got that little piece of paper they call a degree."

Despite the scathing tone, she really did fascinate him.

"Where did you go to school?" he asked.

She crumpled another message and tossed it. "I think you missed my point."

He retrieved it from the floor, fighting against the smile that tugged at his lips. "No, I'm just trying to move beyond the fact that you're obviously annoyed with me for something that wasn't my fault."

"You told Mr. Taka that you wanted me to be your tour guide."

"Yes, but I didn't know he could make it happen. Now that he has, I can't regret it since this may be my only chance to spend time with you."

"You're right about that," she grumbled.

He lowered himself into one of the chairs across from her desk. "Where did you go to journalism school?" he asked again.

"Stanford."

"Impressive."

She shrugged and started shuffling through a pile of faxes from her in-box.

"Where'd you learn to speak Japanese?" he asked.

"Here."

He glanced around the tiny cubicle, raised an eyebrow in silent question.

Finally she smiled. "In Japan. My family moved to Tokyo when I was nine."

"From where?"

"Zurich. Before that we lived in Athens. Before that it was Venice." She frowned. "Or maybe it was Paris and then

Venice. With periodic trips back to the States—New York or Dallas or San Francisco."

"Bet that really racked up the frequent flyer points."

She shrugged again. "My parents like to travel, and their business demands it."

"What's their business?"

"Hotels."

He felt as though a light bulb had clicked on inside his head. "You're *that* Anderson? Of Anderson Hotels?"

"It's the name on my driver's license," she said lightly. "And no, I'm not going to get you a discount on your room."

"I should have guessed. A woman who wears Cartier isn't working as a reporter for the money."

She tugged the sleeve of her blouse over her wrist, tucking the gold watch out of sight. "You are observant."

"That's part of my job," he said.

"And your job is?" she prompted, showing the first sign of interest in his reasons for being there.

"I'm a corporate attorney with Hanson Media Group."

"A lawyer," she said. "Figures."

He frowned. "You have a problem with lawyers?"

"Not lawyers in particular," she said. "Just pushy people in general."

"Pushy?" he tried to sound indignant.

"I'm sure I'm not the first person to bring that particular attribute to your attention," she said dryly.

"No," he admitted. "That would have been my mother when I was about three. Of course, I learned it from her."

She smiled, but it was the hint of sadness in her eyes that intrigued him more than the curve of her lips. There was a story there, he was sure, and damned if he wasn't determined to find out what it was.

"It was my mother's idea for me to become a lawyer," he continued.

"She must be pleased that you did."

There was a time he thought she would have been, too, before his father's death. Since that fateful event, Richard had given up hope that his mother would ever accept the choices he'd made that conflicted with her own agenda.

Although he was glad Jenny was finally participating in the conversation, he wasn't so pleased that she was steering it in a direction he didn't want to follow, reminding him of things he didn't want to remember. "Why don't we get to know each other over coffee?"

"Because I've had enough coffee today and I have work to do if you want me to be available tomorrow."

"Are you?" He smiled again. "Available, that is?"

"I'm not interested, Mr. Warren. That's an entirely different scenario."

"Is it just me—or are you always this prickly?"

"Only when I've had a hard-earned assignment taken away."

"I really didn't intend for that to happen."

She sighed. "Unfortunately that doesn't change the facts."

"Maybe you'll end up with a bigger and better story."

"Maybe." She didn't sound convinced, but then she leaned back in her chair and looked at him. "So you're here to work on the merger."

It wasn't a question, but he nodded anyway.

"How long have you worked for Hanson Media?"

"A little more than a year."

"What happened?"

"What do you mean?" He asked the question warily, but he'd already sensed her agile mind switching gears. She was in investigative mode now, full of questions and searching for answers.

"How did a publishing giant end up on the verge of bankruptcy?" she asked.

"That's a long and complicated story."

"I might be interested in hearing about it over dinner."

As tempted as he was to take the bait she'd dangled, it wasn't an option. "Unfortunately, it's not my story to tell."

"That is unfortunate," she agreed.

"How about dinner, anyway?"

"I don't think so."

He was disappointed though not really surprised by her response. "You're brushing me off because I won't divulge privileged information?"

"I'm merely keeping my schedule open to explore other investigative opportunities," she countered.

"I thought you were a society reporter."

"A temporary assignment," she assured him. "I have bigger ambitions than that."

He'd already concluded as much. "Why don't we talk about those ambitions over dinner?"

She shook her head. "Nice try, though."

"I'm trying to show that I can be persistent as opposed to merely pushy."

"I'll see you tomorrow," she said.

It wasn't quite the response he was hoping for, but he knew it was the most he could expect at this point. He sighed. "What time tomorrow?"

Samara's low whistle of appreciation drew Jenny's focus from Richard's undeniably appealing backside as he walked away.

Her oldest and best friend, and her roommate since she'd returned to Tokyo, perched on the edge of the desk. "Who's the hunk?"

She had to admit it was an apt description for Richard Warren. The dark brown hair, deep blue eyes and quick, easy smile were a combination any woman could appreciate. Add to the equation six feet of height, broad shoulders and narrow hips, and even Jenny was tempted to sigh. But she'd made the mistake of being taken in by good looks and magnetic charm before—it was a mistake she wouldn't make again. "Your so-called hunk is my current nightmare."

Samara's dark eyes sparkled with interest, her lips curved. "Tell me everything."

"Richard Warren, lawyer for Hanson Media Group. He's in town to negotiate terms for a proposed merger with TAKA. And he cost me my byline on the Kakubishi story."

Samara's smile faded. "What? How?"

"By suggesting to Shiguro Taka that he wanted me to show him around town."

"You were pulled off of a front-page assignment for that?"

"Apparently there was some kind of mix-up at the airport and Shiguro Taka is bending over backward to make up for it."

Her friend winced sympathetically. "Who's taking over your story?"

Jenny shrugged. "I don't know, but it makes me furious that I did all the legwork, I sold Lincoln on the story, and now I don't even get to write it."

"I'm sorry, Jenny."

"Not as sorry as I am."

"We could make a trade," Samara suggested. "I'll give you my camera for your hunk."

"As tempted as I am to take you up on that generous offer, I'm not sure Kazuo would appreciate it," she responded dryly.

Samara waved her left hand. "Until he puts a ring on my finger, I'm a cheap agent."

Jenny laughed. "The expression is free agent."

"Whatever." She shrugged. "So what are your plans for Richard Warren?"

She couldn't prevent the smile that tugged at the corner of her lips. "I'm considering a couple of possibilities."

"Uh-oh."

"What?"

"I know that look," Samara said.

"What look?"

"Devious innocence." Her friend's gaze narrowed. "What are you planning?"

Jenny laughed again. "I'm planning to get free of Mr. Warren."

"How?"

"By ensuring that he's so bored after our first day together he won't want to spend any more time with me." She could picture it already—Richard Warren's eyes as glazed as the *chawan* he'd be holding awkwardly in his hands, wishing he'd never approached her outside the shareholders' meeting.

"How?" Samara asked again.

She smiled. "Two words—*tea ceremony.*"

Chapter Two

Tea ceremony?

"A lot of Westerners have the mistaken impression that tea in Japan is simply a pleasant pastime," Jenny told Richard as they exited the subway station. "But *cha-no-yu* is really a spiritual ceremony—a religion of the art of life."

She'd said nothing about their plans for the day until they'd disembarked from the train, promising only that it was an experience Richard wouldn't forget. The way she said it, he wasn't sure it was a good thing. She'd been pleasant and scrupulously polite since meeting him in the lobby of his hotel, but he sensed some residual resentment about the way she'd been coerced into spending time with him.

"There are various forms of the ceremony," she told him. "Even some of the local hotels offer an abbreviated version, but I thought you would enjoy participating in a more authentic celebration."

He tried to hide his skepticism as he listened to her explanation. While a traditional Japanese tea wouldn't have been his first choice of how to spend the day, he was happy to be with her—and only her. Since his arrival in Japan, he'd been shadowed by one or more of TAKA's people and while they were incredibly polite and hospitable, he was tired of constantly being on his best behavior. He wanted to relax for a little while and share unstilted conversation with a pretty woman.

Except that he was getting the impression they wouldn't have much time for casual conversation. Even now, on the way to the teahouse, she was providing a steady flow of information as if she were a professional tour guide. If he'd been seeking company knowledgeable about the culture and history of Japan, he couldn't have chosen anyone better. But what he really wanted was a glimpse into the woman behind the mask of polite reserve.

So far, he'd seen that mask slip only once—yesterday afternoon when Shiguro Taka had appointed her to be his personal tour guide. Since then, she'd seemed to accept her unwelcome fate with stoicism.

"It was a Zen priest who first brought tea to Japan," she informed him. "And the simplicity and purity of the religion was a strong influence on the form of the tea ceremony. But Zen focuses on the enlightenment of the individual through isolation and mediation, and *cha-no-yu* involves the communication of people through spirit and mind."

He watched the subtle sway of her hips as she walked ahead of him, his mind more focused on the urge of his body to communicate with hers than any spiritual matters.

It was a desire he knew would go unsatisfied. Jenny had made it clear that being with him today was nothing more than a command performance, the fulfillment of a professional obligation.

Disappointed though he was, he knew it was for the best. He couldn't afford to have his attention diverted from the task that had brought him to Japan. So he tore his gaze from the enticing curve of her backside as he followed her up the stone path toward a small building made of wooden logs that seemed to be held together with mud.

"Japanese tearooms and gardens are designed to blend harmoniously with their natural surroundings," she explained. "Because the ceremony is linked closely to nature, parts of the ceremony vary according to the season. The flowers displayed, the utensils used, the cakes served."

He watched as she removed her shoes and set them neatly at the entrance. He did the same, then followed her into the building. She set her purse in a woven basket on the porch before turning to him. "Do you have a cell phone?"

He nodded. It wasn't actually his but one that had been loaned to him for his personal use while he was in Japan. He might be frustrated with the delay in negotiations, but he couldn't fault the TAKA people for their gracious hospitality.

"You leave it here—" she gestured to the basket "—in the *yoritsuki*, the entry."

"Leave my cell phone?"

She lifted one perfectly arched brow. "Is that a problem?"

"Of course not. But..." he faltered, wondering how to convey his objection, wondering why he wanted to object. Because he was here on business and he needed to be accessible to Helen. Because he was a lawyer and his cell phone was like a natural appendage.

"You could just turn it off," Jenny said. "But it's more respectful to leave such obvious symbols of the outside world outside of the teahouse."

Despite the nonchalant tone, he sensed a hint of disapproval in her words. He unclipped the phone from his belt even as he wondered why her censure bothered him.

Still, he couldn't resist teasing her. "Do you think I could have coffee instead of tea?"

She turned back, her expression no longer neutral, and he took a perverse sort of pleasure in the sparks in her deep green eyes. "This isn't Starbucks," she said frostily.

"I've just never been much of a tea drinker," he explained.

"Tea is only part of the ceremony," she told him. "It's more about achieving harmony with your host and spiritual satisfaction through silent meditation." She glanced at the cell still clutched in his hand. "If you can't part with your phone for a little while, you're welcome to wait outside."

Although a part of him still balked at being unavailable if Helen needed to get in touch with him, he couldn't refuse her challenge. He turned the phone off and tossed it into the *yoritsuki* with Jenny's purse.

"I wouldn't miss it for the world," he told her.

They were words Richard would regret as soon as he realized there were no other guests for the tea ceremony.

Maybe he should have been flattered that Jenny had arranged a private demonstration, instead he felt as if he were a foreign specimen being examined through a microscope. An apt description as he was foreign to the setting and completely out of his element. Unlike Jenny who was obviously familiar with the customs and rituals.

He tried to follow her lead, bowing when she bowed, kneeling when she knelt. But he remained silent while she made conversation, complimenting their host on the ink painted scroll and the beautiful arrangement of flowers. At least that's what Jenny told him she was saying—as the entire dialogue was in Japanese, he couldn't be sure.

The woman hosting the ceremony was introduced as Izumi. She wore a silk kimono of deep blue patterned with silver fish jumping over it. She was obviously elderly, her hair more gray than black and fashioned into a knot at the back of her neck. Her face was deeply lined, her posture slightly bent, but there was a quiet strength evident in the grace of her movements and a sparkle in her dark eyes befitting a woman half her age.

"Kaiseki," Jenny said, offering no further explanation for the selection of dishes that was set in front of him.

He was both impressed and confused by the elaborate presentation of the food, each item or a small selection of items—most of which he'd never seen before and couldn't have guessed at the names—served on individual dishes. Small glazed bowls, shallow square plates, crescent-shaped dishes, miniature cups for sauces and garnishes. Growing up, Richard could only remember eating salad from a separate dish if there was company at the dinner table. Otherwise, his mother insisted the greens went on the same plate as the rest of the meal.

He wondered if that was still true. It had been so long since he'd had a meal in her home, he was no longer certain. With the thought came a sharp but now familiar pang of regret. He'd lost his father almost ten years ago and his mother had distanced herself shortly after that, more concerned with putting her husband's killer behind bars than maintaining a relationship with her sons.

Izumi spoke softly to him, interrupting the painful memories of his past and returning his attention to the present. Unfortunately, his Japanese vocabulary was too limited to even attempt a translation.

"She asked if you're enjoying your *sunomono,*" Jenny told him.

He assumed she meant the grated vegetables he'd just sampled. *"Oishii,"* he responded. Delicious.

Izumi smiled and placed yet another series of dishes in front of him.

Jenny, he noticed, seemed annoyed rather than pleased by his reply. And he was starting to suspect that she hadn't brought him here to enjoy the ceremony but because she expected that he'd be bored by it. Rather than be offended by the realization, he was only more intrigued. As interesting as the rituals of the tea ceremony were, he found his reluctant companion even more so.

In his thirty-four years, he'd indulged in several casual affairs and a few more serious relationships. He'd even been married once. But he couldn't ever remember feeling the kind of basic pull toward a woman that tugged at him now.

Unfortunately, he was in Tokyo for the merger and she worked—however indirectly—for TAKA. While a personal relationship might not result in a direct conflict of interest, it would complicate the situation for both of them.

Besides, she didn't strike him as the type of woman to indulge in brief affairs and he wasn't going to be in Tokyo long enough to offer her anything else.

So resolved, he decided to use this time of contemplation to refocus his thoughts, mentally organize his questions and concerns about the merger. He was annoyed to find that his thoughts refused to focus.

In the past his attention had always strayed to work and work-related issues, but this time he found his attention straying to the woman beside him. While he allowed himself the occasional distraction of a woman—of his choosing and on his timetable—he'd never allowed himself to be distracted *by* a woman. And the women he'd chosen had always been those more interested in blowing off a little steam than a relationship, and that had always suited him fine.

Since his divorce, shallow and temporarily satisfying interludes were all he'd wanted or needed. Until a few months ago when he'd crawled out from between the silk sheets of a district court judge with whom he'd spent the night and suddenly wondered if that was all he could hope for in his life.

Izumi's gentle voice interrupted his thoughts.

"She noticed that you're frowning," Jenny told him.

"Sorry," he apologized automatically. *"Sumimasen."*

"Don't be sorry," Jenny translated as their hostess measured some kind of green powder into a bowl. "Be at peace. Clear your mind of disturbing thoughts. Relax."

Easy to say but impossible to do when the source of the disturbance was so close—and his thoughts about her were anything but relaxing.

Jenny felt Richard's gaze on her. She was conscious of his attention, of everything about him, though she wished she wasn't. And she was annoyed with herself that she'd so obviously underestimated him.

She really hadn't expected that he would still be here.

In her experience, career-driven men didn't appreciate the opportunity to sit down and relax for five minutes, never mind five hours. She knew for certain that her ex wouldn't have lasted this long—Brad was too restless and edgy to ever completely unwind. Maybe that was one of the reasons they were so fundamentally wrong for each other. Or maybe she was only looking for reasons now that they'd gone their separate ways.

It had been her choice to end their relationship, and as she hadn't seen or heard from him in the six months that had since passed, she found it strange that she was thinking of him now. Or maybe the thought was a warning from her subconscious. Because while there was no more than a surface resemblance between Brad and Richard, she couldn't help but feel they were alike on the inside. Brad's only thought had been the next story; Richard was—even now, she imagined—preoccupied by the merger between Hanson Media and TAKA.

She needed to remember that single-minded drive and forget about the tingles that danced through her veins whenever he looked at her. No matter how strong the attraction between them, she wasn't going to play second fiddle to any man's career again. She had her own hopes and dreams and she wasn't going to be sidetracked.

On the other hand, she wasn't going to let her ambitions dictate the course of her life, either. She believed in balance and harmony—it was one of the reasons she loved the tea ceremony. The serenity and history were as important to her as the ritual preparation and sharing of food and drink.

She'd needed that serenity today. As annoyed as she'd been about losing her assignment, she relished the time for silent meditation, the opportunity to purge the negative emotions from her soul. The fact that the very same rituals were likely boring Richard Warren to tears was merely an added bonus. He might be graciously enduring the ceremony, but she would bet that after it was over, he'd be not just willing but eager to undertake the rest of his sightseeing alone. Or at least without her.

She felt a brief prick of guilt, released it with a long slow breath. She had no reason to feel guilty. If the American lawyer was too uptight to relax and enjoy one of the cornerstones of Japanese culture, she could hardly be held responsible.

"It didn't work, you know."

They were the first words Richard spoke to Jenny upon exiting the teahouse.

"What didn't work?" she asked, feigning innocence.

"Using the tea ceremony to convince me to find another tour guide."

"I'd hoped you would enjoy it," she lied. "*Cha-no-yu* is a fascinating part of Japanese culture."

His smile was quick, easy and completely disarming. "Then you weren't hoping to bore me to death?"

She felt her own lips start to curve, fought to keep her expression neutral as she turned down the path leading away from the tea house. "Mr. Taka would never forgive me if I was responsible for the demise of an honored guest."

"And if you could do away with me without risk of any professional repercussions?" he asked, falling into step beside her.

"They'd never find your body."

He laughed. "That's what I thought."

This time she let the smile come. "You're a good sport, Mr. Warren."

"Richard," he corrected. "And I had a good time."

"I'm glad," she said, surprised to realize it was true. Although her original intention had been thwarted, she found she wasn't disappointed. She didn't know many men—and none who weren't Japanese—who could relax and enjoy the traditional ceremony that she loved. It made her wonder if she might have been too quick in her judgment of him.

Or maybe not.

As he clipped his cell phone back onto his belt, she reminded herself that he was a lawyer in town on temporary business. Definitely not a man her fickle heart should be weaving any romantic fantasies about. She knew only too well that the charm and attentiveness would dissipate in an instant when the demands of the job called.

"You seemed to know Izumi quite well," he said.

Obviously he'd been paying more attention than she'd given him credit for. "She's my roommate's great-grandmother."

"You have a roommate?"

She smiled at the surprise evident in his question. "You apparently have no idea how expensive rent is in Tokyo."

"But your parents are Anderson Hotels."

"They are," she agreed. "I'm not."

"Why not? Surely there must be numerous career opportunities for you within the family organization."

"I wanted to be a reporter."

"And that was okay with them?" he asked.

"They weren't thrilled with my choice at first, but they've always supported me."

"You're lucky."

She nodded. It was what she reminded herself every day—she *was* incredibly fortunate to have parents who loved and stood by her. Unfortunately that knowledge couldn't silence the questions or lessen the pain that came from not having been wanted by the woman who'd given her away only a few hours after giving birth to her.

"You were telling me about Izumi," he reminded her.

"Why are you so interested?"

"She seemed like an interesting woman," he said. "Someone who's lived a satisfying life, with a sparkle in her eyes that suggests she's not nearly finished living it yet."

Again, he'd surprised her. And because he'd so clearly understood the woman who was dear to her own heart, Jenny couldn't help softening toward him.

"She would love that description," she admitted.

"You're close to her," he guessed.

She nodded. "I don't have any grandparents of my own, but I spent enough time at Samara's when we were kids that Izumi became like a grandmother to me.

"But long before she was a grandmother, she was a geisha," she told him. "It was while working as a geisha that she met and fell in love with Samara's great-grandfather. They got married three weeks after their first meeting and had four children together before he went off to war. He never came back."

Jenny had cried the first time she heard the story and almost every time since. Especially when Izumi told it— the emotion in her voice reflecting her love and grief as clearly as if it had been a recent loss, not something that had happened many years ago.

"She said that when she learned of his death, she felt as though a part of her had died, too. Then her baby—Samara's grandfather—cried to be fed, and she realized she hadn't lost him completely. So long as she had her children, she would always have part of him."

It had made Jenny realize that she wanted the same thing—to love and be loved, deeply and forever, to have a family of her own and children who were part of herself as no one else was.

"It's a beautiful story," he said. "Almost enough to make the most cynical person believe in true love."

"Almost?"

He shrugged.

"I'm guessing you would be that most cynical person."

"Let's just say that my experience has been different."

"Every experience is, as Izumi would agree." She turned to Richard and smiled. "She married three more times."

"So much for true love."

She shook her head. "You are a cynic."

"Four marriages is a lot by any standards."

"What's your standard? How many did it take to destroy your faith in love?"

"Just one marriage and one divorce."

"And you have no intention of trying again," she guessed.

"I like to think I'm smart enough to have learned my lesson the first time."

"Izumi's situation is different. She didn't divorce her husbands, she buried them. And I think her willingness to still believe in love is admirable. Of course, being widowed three times might explain why she's currently married to a man almost twenty years her junior." She smiled again. "It might also explain the sparkle in her eye."

The glimpse of humor caught him off guard and completely captivated him. She was relaxed now, her defenses seemingly forgotten as she stopped trying to keep him at a distance and really talked to him.

When he'd first seen her across the room at TAKA yesterday, he'd been struck by her looks—both the uncanny sense of recognition and the cool, poised beauty. Now, with her eyes soft and her lips curved, the sun shining down on her, she was warm and real and infinitely more appealing.

The attraction he'd felt from the first stirred again, more insistently this time. Richard reminded himself that he had a lot of valid reasons for keeping things casual and only one for making a move—he wanted her. But that want was starting to prove a more powerful force than logic.

"What would it take," he wondered aloud, "to put that kind of sparkle in your eye?"

Her smile didn't fade, but there was no doubt it cooled. "More than you'd be willing to give," she said in a level tone.

"Now that sounds like a challenge."

"It's not—just a fact."

"You're determined not to like me, aren't you?"

"I don't dislike you, Mr. Warren. I just have no interest in being a diversion for a guy like you."

"A guy like me?" He felt his irritation mounting. "What does that mean?"

"You're good-looking, charming and successful."

How, he wondered, did she manage to make the statement so that it flattered and insulted at the same time?

"And because you have time on your hands," she continued, "you assume any woman you want should be willing to help you fill it."

He scowled, not just because of the accusation but because he realized there was some truth in what she'd said. He'd seen her, wanted her and gone after her.

"I'm a novelty for you—a woman who isn't falling at your feet."

"I've never actually had to step over the bodies," he said dryly. "But I've also never met a woman so obviously opposed to my company."

She met his gaze evenly. "I have no intention of being your plaything for the few weeks that you're going to be in town."

"Well, that's certainly blunt."

"I just want to make sure there are no misunderstandings."

"For your information, I'm not in the habit of pursuing a woman who's made it clear that she's not interested."

"Then there shouldn't be a problem."

She started to walk away.

He grabbed her arm and turned her back to face him. "Except I'm not convinced you're not interested."

Chapter Three

Jenny wanted to be annoyed by his arrogance, except she knew that he was right. His fingers slid down her arm to her wrist, his slow smile confirming that he'd registered the skip and race of her pulse. She could find all kinds of words to deny the attraction between them, but she couldn't deny her physical response to him.

"Tell me that you don't want me to kiss you," he said, his lips hovering mere inches above hers.

Right now, with his body so close to hers she could feel his heat and hear his heart pound, she wanted his kiss more than she wanted to take her next breath. And that was precisely why she couldn't let it happen. Wanting anything from a man like Richard Warren could only lead to heartache. So she opened her mouth to voice the denial—even if it was a lie.

Before she could speak a single word, he kissed her.

At the first touch of his lips, desire swept over her in an unexpected and overpowering wave. Recognizing the futility of struggling against it, she let herself flow with it—the deep, almost desperate need.

His arm banded around her waist, holding her tight against him so she couldn't pull away. Heat seared her body everywhere it touched his. Her breasts, her hips, her thighs. Too much heat. It was impossible to even think of pulling away when she was melting against him.

She laid her palms on his chest, felt the quick, steady beat of his heart. Her own was pumping to the same rhythm, her blood pulsing heavily in her veins. Her hands slid over the hard contour of muscle to link behind his neck, holding on, as any protests she might have uttered turned into desires and her subconscious denials became needs.

His hand stroked up her back, the bold touch shooting arrows of pleasure through her. Then he cupped her neck to tilt her head back, his fingers sifting through her hair.

Again, he surprised her. Instead of deepening the kiss, the pressure of his mouth gentled. His lips moved away from hers to trail soft kisses along the line of her jaw. He nibbled gently on her ear, cruised slowly down her throat. Featherlight caresses that whispered over her skin.

He was no longer taking but giving, and Jenny couldn't refuse what he was offering. She didn't know how to fight against such tender passion. She didn't want to. She trembled against him, her body quivering with desire.

"Richard."

When she spoke his name, it was a sigh, a plea.

His mouth moved back to hers. Slowly, patiently, he took

her deeper. It was like a dream—soft and warm and misty, with just the hint of danger hovering around the edges.

His tongue slid between her parted lips, skimmed over hers. She welcomed him, felt rather than heard the soft whimper deep in her own throat.

She tried to tell herself that she didn't want this. She knew she *shouldn't* want this. But reason and logic had abandoned her, and she only wanted him.

Richard had intended to make a point—to force Jenny to acknowledge the attraction between them. He hadn't expected that he'd end up wanting so much more. He eased his mouth from hers with unexpected reluctance and drew in a desperate lungful of air and willed his mind to clear, his thoughts to focus. Then he made the mistake of looking at her again.

Her lips were still swollen from his kiss, her eyes still cloudy with desire, her body still soft and warm against his. He felt an almost overwhelming urge to kiss her again, to take everything she didn't seem to realize she was offering.

It was the obvious vulnerability and the almost imperceptible hint of fear in her eyes that held his passion in check. He didn't know what she was afraid of, but he knew she was smart to be afraid. Whatever was happening between them was too much too fast—they both needed to take a step back.

"It seems as though you were right about my interest," he murmured. "And wrong about your own."

She opened her mouth, probably to argue the point, then closed it again. They both knew it was absurd to protest when she was still in his arms.

"It doesn't change anything," she said. "I'm not going to sleep with you."

He wondered if she was aware of the tremor in her own voice, or how incredibly arousing it was to know he'd been the one to shake her cool poise. So arousing that he was tempted to interpret her words as another challenge and set upon changing her mind. But he'd been as shaken as she by the kiss they'd shared, and he decided it might be wise to accept the boundaries she was setting—at least for now.

"All right," he agreed. "No sleeping together on the first date."

She narrowed her eyes. "This isn't a date."

"Does that mean we can sleep together?"

"No." Her response was firm, but he saw the smile tugging at the corner of her lips in response to his teasing.

It had been his intent to lessen the tension, but the hint of a smile had drawn his attention back to her mouth, tempting him to kiss her again.

He tore his gaze away. "Okay, then. What's next on the agenda?"

She hesitated, as if she didn't trust the easy compliance his question suggested. "How about the theater?"

"That sounds great," he said.

A theater would at least be filled with people and the action on the stage might keep his attention focused—and away from the temptation of his tour guide.

The theater had seemed like a good idea when she'd first decided upon it. Jenny had been certain that a few more hours of inactivity after the lengthy tea ceremony would be more than enough to drive Richard to abandon her company completely. Of course, that was *before* the kiss.

The kiss she should never have allowed to happen. But now that it had, there was no way to pretend it away, and no denying her response to him. And as she sat beside him in the dark, every nerve ending in her body was painfully attuned to his nearness.

She tried to remain immobile, her gaze focused on the stage. She didn't remember the seats seeming so close. Or maybe it was that Richard was so tall. But every time he shifted in his seat, which he did frequently, his shoulder brushed hers or his thigh pressed against hers. The disproportionate response of her own body to these casual touches reminded her that it had been a long time since she'd had sex.

Not that she intended to sleep with Richard Warren. Certainly not after spending only one day with him. *No way.* She was definitely through with single-minded men and dead-end relationships.

The thought faded away as his knee bumped against her leg again.

She'd often thought it was more of a curse than a blessing that she enjoyed sex. Her relationship with Brad had lacked a lot of things, but she had no complaints about the physical aspects of it. Maybe that was why she'd waited so long to end a relationship she'd recognized was at an impasse months earlier. Or maybe it was because she'd really wanted him to be the one.

She'd made excuses for his frequent disappearances and hasty departures. He was an investigative reporter and traveling was part of his job. She'd known that when they'd first started dating and could hardly expect him to change his career for her.

She had hoped he would want to make *some* changes, though. To talk to her before making his travel plans rather than calling from a plane that was already in the air.

But Brad had become accustomed to flying solo long before she'd ever moved in with him, and she'd been too afraid to sound like a nagging wife to make an issue of it. She'd gratefully accepted the part of his life he was willing to share with her because she'd believed it was preferable to being alone.

Two and a half years later, she'd realized that she was alone even when she was sleeping beside him. She'd finally accepted that he would always want the next big headline more than he wanted her.

Always being second best hurt more than she wanted to admit—even more so because he wasn't the first man in her life to put his career ahead of her. With James it had been his research; Kevin his music. Richard, for all his current attentiveness, wouldn't be any different. He was looking for a temporary diversion, and she had no intention of being one.

Or maybe she was looking at the situation from the wrong perspective. Maybe spending time with him was the most effective way to prove he was the same as the other men she'd dated. That would certainly kill any attraction she felt.

His thigh brushed against hers again and her hormones exploded like a Fourth of July fireworks display. She definitely needed to get past this physical pull, learn more about him, find his faults. Because if she ever gave in to the traitorous desire pumping through her veins, she would end up with her heart broken all over again.

Richard wasn't answering his phone.

Helen Hanson paced the confines of her office, gnawing on her bottom lip as the long-distance ring sounded again before finally connecting to his voice mail.

She hung up without leaving a message. She'd left three already.

She pushed away from her desk and stared out at the array of lights blinking below her. It was four o'clock in the afternoon in Tokyo and she'd been trying to reach him for hours. Where could he be?

He'd given her a cell phone number so that she could keep in touch, but that wasn't happening.

She knew he wasn't in a meeting. He'd called yesterday to tell her the start of negotiations had been delayed. One of TAKA's key executives had been called out of town because of a death in the family.

She knew only too well how the loss of a loved one could send a person's entire world into turmoil. Six months after burying her husband, she still felt as though she was swirling in a vortex of confusion.

She'd loved George dearly, but if by some miracle he could be standing before her now, she'd cheerfully throttle him for making such a mess of the company that should have been a legacy for his children. Instead it had been— to varying degrees—a curse.

Of course, if the company had been the financial success he'd led them all to believe, none of his sons would be where they were right now.

Jack had put his legal career and his own ambitions on hold to help out at Hanson. In the process, he'd been reacquainted and fallen in love with Samantha Edwards, whom he'd first met years ago when they were in business school together. Helen smiled, thinking that she deserved at least a little bit of credit for that match, as she'd been the one to suggest Samantha to Jack as a viable candidate to lead the Internet division.

Andrew, a typical rich playboy before his father's death, had reluctantly returned to Chicago to assume some responsibility at Hanson Media Group. In doing so, he'd come face-to-face with a former one-night stand who was pregnant with his child. Now he and Delia McCray were happily married and looking forward to parenthood together.

Evan's journey had, perhaps, been the most difficult. Cut out of his father's will, he'd almost turned away from the family business completely. Fortunately, Helen had managed to convince him to stay—at least for a while—and he'd reunited with Meredith Waters. Although the former high school sweethearts were still working out some of the kinks in their new relationship, Helen knew they were committed to one another.

Yes, she thought with satisfaction, George's sons all had reason to be grateful rather than angry with their father.

But what about me? She couldn't help but wonder.

What had George left her except controlling interest in an almost bankrupt company and the resentment of his children who were now working for her?

She hated knowing that the boys thought of her as nothing more than a trophy wife. She resented that George had let them believe it, and she was disappointed with herself for letting him make her into one.

She hadn't minded so much when he was alive. She'd loved George and being his wife had given her life both purpose and pleasure. His death had taken those away—along with her illusions.

Sometimes she wondered why she was even still here, trying so desperately to hold together the business that he'd let fall apart. But she knew it was what she needed to do—it was the only way she could prove to herself that the last ten years of her life had served any purpose. That was why she was so desperate for this merger to work.

She picked up the phone to try Richard again, then hung it up without dialing. While she had every confidence that he could handle the negotiations, she felt anxious being so far removed from the action. Maybe she should go to Tokyo herself. If nothing else, a change of scenery might help her put everything into perspective.

Richard should have guessed Jenny would pick a sushi restaurant for dinner when his mouth was watering for a thick juicy steak.

When in Rome, he reminded himself. Except that in Rome he'd be more likely looking at a bowl of noodles with a chunky marinara sauce than cold fish wrapped in seaweed, and he loved pasta.

Not that he disliked sushi so much as he disliked the idea of sushi. His ex-wife had, on several occasions, tried to entice Richard to try it. It had never appealed to him. Then again, Marilyn had indulged in a lot of things he never had—and while he could accept her liking of unusual foods, he couldn't overlook her infidelity.

Jenny stopped in front of an illuminated window display that showcased the restaurant's menu. Richard stared at the assortment of plastic food searching for anything that looked the least bit appealing. Each dish had a label—in Japanese, of course—and a number.

"What do you think?" she asked.

"I think I'd like meat—preferably cooked."

She smiled. "Have you ever tried sushi?"

He shook his head. "The thought of eating anything raw, other than vegetables, does not appeal to me."

"Today is a day for experiencing new things," she reminded him. "The tea ceremony, *Noh* theater."

"That seems like enough new experiences for awhile."

"And just when I thought you had an adventurous side."

"Do I really have to eat sushi to prove I'm not a straight-laced conservative?"

"You don't have to prove anything to me," she told him.

Of course, he ordered the sushi. Rather, he told Jenny what he wanted and let her order for him.

Tekka-maki, she explained, was cold, vinegary rice wrapped with tuna in a sheet of toasted seaweed. The description was innocuous if not exactly appealing.

She ordered something called *kappa-maki* and, when their meals were delivered, she demonstrated the proper way to pick up the roll with the chopsticks and dip it into the sauce.

He followed her example and was both surprised and relieved to find the *maki-zushi* was quite enjoyable—pleasantly tangy with the slightest hint of salt and not at all fishy.

Richard lifted his glass of beer. "Thank you," he said. "For a day filled with new experiences."

Jenny raised her own drink. *"Kampai."* Cheers.

It was there again—something in the tilt of her chin, the slight curve of her lips that nagged at him. "Do you have a sister?"

She frowned at the question as she shook her head. "Just a brother."

"Cousins?"

"A few. Why?"

"Because I still can't shake the feeling that you remind me of someone."

"I thought that was just a line," she admitted.

"If I needed one, I could do better than that."

"Yes, I imagine you could," she responded in a tone that challenged the obsequiousness of her words.

She picked up another *maki-zushi* and dipped it.

"Do you have any family in Chicago?" he pressed.

"Not that I know of." She popped the roll into her mouth.

He studied her as he sipped his beer, wondering why she intrigued him so much. It wasn't just the physical attraction or the nagging familiarity, although those were certainly factors. Her intelligence and passion were definite pluses but not the whole answer, either. It was, he finally realized, the whole package that had caught and held his attention. And it was the whole woman he wanted.

He frowned at the thought and reminded himself he wasn't looking for a woman or any kind of personal complications right now.

"You're not eating," Jenny said. "Is your dinner okay?"

He shoved the discomfiting thoughts aside and picked up another piece of fish. "It's fine. I guess my mind wandered."

"Are you thinking about the merger?"

He *should* have been thinking about the merger. Instead, he'd been contemplating a union of an entirely different sort. "Something like that."

"You must be frustrated with the delay."

"A little," he admitted. "Although Helen is even more so. Patience isn't one of her virtues."

"Helen?" she prompted.

"Helen Hanson."

Jenny thought it interesting that he was on a first name basis with his boss. Not that their relationship—business or personal—was any of her concern. Still, she couldn't help prying just a little. "She must think very highly of you to have entrusted you to work out the details of the merger."

"She's a savvy businessperson," he said. Then he smiled. "She's also a good friend."

"I didn't ask," she said.

"But you were wondering."

She shrugged. "I saw her picture in the paper and on the news—when her husband was buried. Although she was wearing big sunglasses that obscured half of her face, it was still obvious that she's a beautiful woman. Beautiful and young."

"Are you looking for a story?"

"Just making conversation."

"Then I'll tell you that she's an incredible person who's managing to hold a troubled company together while still mourning her husband's death."

"Why do you think she's doing it?" Jenny couldn't help but ask. "Why would she care about saving Hanson Media when it's obvious none of her stepsons appreciates her efforts?"

"Only Helen could answer that for certain," he told her.

She shook her head. "They don't know how lucky they are that their father's wife wants to be involved in their lives. There are women who don't want the responsibility of their own children, never mind someone else's." Women like her own mother, who had abandoned her at birth and disappeared from her life completely.

"That's an interesting way of looking at it."

Jenny shrugged to hide the fact that she was uneasy with his sudden scrutiny, concerned that her impulsive comment had revealed too much.

"It's an interesting situation." She sipped her drink. "A business crisis with elements of drama and intrigue."

"Are you a reporter or a novelist?"

"I'm just innately curious."

"So am I," he said. "And I've noticed how adeptly you maneuver every conversation away from questions about you to more impersonal topics."

"That's because my life isn't very interesting."

"You left New York City for a job in Tokyo. I find that very interesting."

"My family's here," she said simply. "My parents, my brother and his wife and their four-year-old daughter."

"No boyfriend?"

She realized she'd been so intent on sidestepping one uncomfortable topic she hadn't seen he was maneuvering her toward another.

"I'll assume there's no boyfriend," he continued, "because I don't think you would have kissed me the way you did if there was."

Jenny was quiet for a moment. "I think we need to clear the air about that," she said at last.

"Are you saying there *is* a boyfriend?"

"I'm saying that I didn't mean to give you the wrong impression. I'm attracted to you." She smiled wryly. "Obviously. But I don't do casual relationships. I can't seem to separate the physical from the emotional, and things inevitably get messy."

"I try to avoid messy if at all possible."

She nodded, understanding that it was a warning as much as a confession and was grateful for his honesty.

"But it's not always possible," he told her.

"We'll keep things simple."

He seemed to consider her suggestion for a moment before nodding. "Simple," he agreed. He reached across the table to touch the back of her hand. "Does that mean I can't kiss you good-night?"

She pulled her hand away. "It means no more kissing at all."

"That's a pretty strict position to take."

"It's smart." And necessary. Because she knew that if he kissed her again, all her resolutions about keeping it simple would dissolve like *matcha*—powdered tea—in boiling water.

"All right—no kissing. Simple. Smart. Are there any other rules I should know about?"

He was teasing her, trying to lessen the tension.

She smiled to hide the fact that she was just the slightest bit disappointed that he'd given in to her demands so readily.

"That should be good for now," she said lightly. "And I should be getting home."

"Do you have a curfew?"

"No, but I have a roommate who worries when she doesn't know where I am." And although Samara knew she was spending the day with Richard, Jenny was afraid that knowledge would only cause her friend to have more questions.

"I'll take you home," he told her.

"You don't know where I live."

He shrugged. "I figure this is a good way to find out."

"Your hotel's closer than my apartment," she pointed out as they left the restaurant. "There's no reason for you to see me home."

"I want to be sure you make it there safely."

"Tokyo is an extremely safe city."

"This is *my* rule," he said. "If we spend the day together, even if it's not a date, I see you home."

"It's really not necessary." She felt silly standing on the sidewalk arguing about it, so she began to walk. "And this is a confusing city to navigate if you're unfamiliar with it. You could get lost trying to find your way back."

"I'll manage."

She didn't try to dissuade him any more, and they walked in silence for several blocks until they reached her apartment building.

"This is it," she said, stopping on the sidewalk.

"Now I'll rest easier knowing my tour guide made it home safely."

She smiled reluctantly. "You still want me to be your tour guide?"

"Absolutely," he answered without hesitation.

"Then I guess I'll see you tomorrow."

"Any hints about what we'll be doing?"

"I'll think about it," she said. "Unless there was anything in particular you wanted to see."

He shook his head. "You're in charge."

She tilted her head back to look at him. "I have to admit, I did expect you would have found an excuse to part ways with me long before now."

"You're surprised by my perseverance?"

"Yes," she admitted.

"Good." He tapped his finger lightly against her chin. "I like knowing that I can surprise you."

She took a step back. "Good night."

"Good night, Jenny."

As she walked inside the building, grateful they'd established an understanding of the rules, Richard watched her, already thinking about breaking them.

Chapter Four

Jenny should have known Samara would be waiting for her. When she opened the door of her apartment, she found her roommate in the living room, thumbing through the pages of a decorating magazine.

Samara glanced up, then at the clock on the wall. "Must have been quite the tea ceremony."

"It was." Jenny dropped her purse and keys on the table.

A moment of silence passed, a few more pages turned before Samara finally asked, "Am I going to have to pry for details?"

Jenny carried two cans of soda from the fridge, passed one to her friend, then popped the top on the other. "I wouldn't know what to tell you," she admitted. "Except that Richard Warren isn't quite who I thought he would be."

Samara closed the magazine and set it aside. "Do you like him?"

"It's too soon to say."

"You just spent the last twelve hours with him—I'd think you'd have an opinion."

She hesitated before admitting, "I enjoyed his company."

"Why do you sound surprised?"

"Because he's smart and charming and far too good-looking."

She was aware that her protests sounded ridiculous, but she also knew that Samara would understand.

Her friend's response confirmed that she did. "He's not Brad Morgan or Kevin Hicks or James Gillett—"

"I know. But he's not that different from any of them either." And she knew that if she ignored her better judgment and let herself get involved with Richard, he would break her heart, too.

"You always said you had great memories of James," Samara reminded her.

"Yeah." Jenny smiled. She'd been twenty years old and completely inexperienced when she'd met James Gillett, and the instant attraction between them had both intrigued and terrified her. He'd been her first love—and her first lover.

"What went wrong?" her friend asked. "Why did you break up with him?"

"Because I finally realized he wasn't ever going to be what I needed, that he wasn't capable of making a commitment." She sighed. "At least that's what I thought until I heard he got married last year."

"James is married?" Samara sounded as stunned as Jenny had been.

She nodded. "Her name's Meghan—she's a doctor."

"You never told me he got married."

"It never came up in conversation."

"If you were pained by it, you should have brought it up."

Her friend's comment made Jenny smile. Although Samara was fluent in English, she still occasionally mixed up similar words. "Why would it bother me?"

"Because you loved him once," Samara said gently.

"Okay, maybe it did bother me a little." She got up to toss her empty can in the garbage. "Or maybe what bothered me was realizing how much I want to be the center of someone's world, like Meghan is for James."

Samara shook her head. "You've been listening to my great-grandmother's stories again."

"She managed to find four men who put her first. All I want is one."

"Some day you'll find him," Samara said, then she smiled. "Or maybe you already have."

Jenny ignored the deliberate hint in the second part of her friend's statement. "Maybe the problem isn't the men," she said. "Maybe it's me. Maybe I'm just not the type of woman who inspires that kind of passion."

"You can't honestly believe that."

"Everyone warned me that James would never commit to one woman. It turns out he just didn't want to commit to me.

"Kevin claimed to love me, then he decided he'd rather be playing his guitar in smoky bars than building a life with me.

"When Brad asked me to move in with him, I thought it was proof we were in a committed relationship. Now I have to wonder if he just wanted someone to water his plants while he was away."

It was the story of her life—always coming in a distant second to someone or something else. And it wasn't just recent experiences that made her feel that way. No, the first seeds of the doubts and insecurities were planted almost twenty-five years earlier when she'd first come into the world and her own mother hadn't even wanted her.

"You've made a few bad choices," Samara said with a shrug. "Who hasn't?"

"Spoken like a true friend." Jenny managed a smile. "But the fact is, not many women have my appalling judgment when it comes to men."

And yet she continued to be drawn to the same type— self-confident and self-absorbed. Men who were not just committed to their careers but obsessed with success, more interested in getting ahead than being with her.

"Maybe Richard's different," Samara said.

She laughed. "Yeah. He's a lawyer instead of a professor, musician or journalist. That doesn't make him any less obsessed with his career."

"He probably bored you to tears talking about legal presidents all day."

"Precedents," Jenny corrected automatically. "And just because he managed to restrain himself from talking law while we were out doesn't mean he wasn't thinking about it."

"You're probably right," Samara agreed, a smile tugging at the corners of her mouth.

Jenny narrowed her gaze on her friend.

"If you want a man who can't think of anything but you, you should date Kimiyasu in circulation. He trips over his tongue every time you walk past his desk."

"He trips over his tongue every time he sees anyone in a skirt," Jenny pointed out.

"Okay, maybe not Kimiyasu. But you should be going out, meeting people."

"I do go out, and I already know a lot of people."

"I meant men," Samara said.

"I know you did—I'm just not interested in dating anyone right now."

"But you're attracted to Richard," Samara guessed.

Her thoughts drifted again to the sizzling kiss they'd shared, and she sighed. "A woman would have to be dead to not be attracted to Richard."

Her friend grinned. "I was beginning to wonder. You haven't dated at all since you moved to Tokyo. And I know it hasn't been from lack of offers."

"I've been busy."

"You've been hiding. Or maybe you've been waiting for Brad to come back."

"If I was waiting for him, I'd still be in New York." Jenny shook her head decisively. "I'm getting on with my life."

"Then why are you so deposed to spending time with Richard Warren? Maybe even having a little fling?"

"Opposed," she said. "And not wanting to jump into bed with another man doesn't mean I'm still hung up on my ex."

"Hmm." Samara propped her feet up on the coffee table, one delicate ankle crossed over the other. "I think the problem isn't that you're not ready to jump into bed with him, but that you are."

She remained silent.

"You're not denying it."

"I'm trying to figure out how many negatives there were in that statement to decipher what you said."

"You want to sleep with Richard, but you know that if you do, you won't be able to go back to Brad."

"I don't want to go back to Brad."

"I bet Richard would be great in bed," Samara continued as if Jenny hadn't spoken.

That was a bet Jenny wasn't willing to take. If his kiss was any indication, Richard wouldn't be great in bed—he would be phenomenal. But she had no intention of telling her friend about the kiss, so all she said was, "That's quite an assumption to make considering that you saw him for all of two minutes."

"What can I say?" Her roommate shrugged. "The man makes an impression."

Jenny couldn't deny the truth of that, either.

Richard did get lost trying to find his way back to his hotel. Although he wasn't entirely sure if it was the lack of recognizable street signs that was responsible for his misdirection or the confusion in his own mind. Because as much as he tried to concentrate on where he was going, he continued to be preoccupied with thoughts of Jenny.

He hadn't realized how structured and predictable his life had become until she'd provided a respite—however temporary—from the tedium of his existence. She intrigued him and challenged him, and she made him feel something he hadn't felt in a very long time—alive.

He wasn't surprised by the attraction he felt. He was surprised that he couldn't seem to put that attraction aside. He'd always managed to divide his life into neat sections: work, family, social. With an admittedly heavy emphasis on work, especially in recent years.

But now he was thinking about Jenny instead of the Hanson-TAKA merger. He was wandering the streets of downtown Tokyo instead of hurrying back to his hotel to review his notes and check his e-mail. And although he'd

left her not thirty minutes ago, he was already looking
forward to tomorrow when he would see her again.

His thoughts strayed again to the steamy kiss they'd
shared in the garden outside of the tea house.

He hadn't planned to kiss her. He'd thought about it—
every time his gaze had lingered on the soft fullness of her
mouth—but he'd had no intention of acting upon his desire.
Until she'd told him to back off in that cool voice that con-
tradicted the heat in her eyes.

It had been an impulse, driven by the need to know
which part of her was real.

It had also been a mistake.

Not because he hadn't enjoyed kissing her, but because
he'd enjoyed it too much. While he'd suspected there was
a lot more to Jenny Anderson than she let most people see,
he hadn't expected so much. The depth and intensity of her
response had surprised him, proving there was passion
beneath the poise and a lot more hot than cool.

He also hadn't expected the wariness he'd seen in her
eyes after the kiss had ended. It was that hint of uncertainty
that held his own desire in check. He liked women with experience, who wanted only the same things he did. For all
her elegance and sophistication, there was a vulnerability
about Jenny Anderson that warned him to proceed with
caution—or not at all.

She was the type of woman who would want more than
he could give her, and he refused to put himself in the
position of disappointing her. He'd already failed his
mother and his wife—he wouldn't set up anyone else for
the same disillusionment.

So he would do the smart thing—he would respect her

wishes and keep their relationship simple. But taking the smart and easy route wouldn't stop him from wanting her.

Thankfully, he would only have to resist temptation for a few more days. As soon as Mr. Tetsugoro was back and negotiations commenced, Richard was confident he would be able to put Jenny Anderson in the back of his mind.

This thought gave him a measure of relief, as did the realization he'd finally found his way back to the hotel.

When he got up to his room, he saw the message light on his phone was blinking. He punched in the code to retrieve his voice mail and found there wasn't just one but four messages waiting—all of them from the acting CEO of Hanson Media Group.

At 10:30 a.m.:

"Hi, Richard, it's Helen. I just thought I'd try to catch you in your room. Obviously you're out, so I'll try the cell phone number you gave me."

11:30 a.m.:

"Richard, it's me again. I tried your cell and immediately was patched through to voice mail. Give me a call when you get this message, please."

2:00 p.m.:

"It isn't like you to be out of touch for so long, Richard. Call me before I really start to worry."

And at 7:30 p.m.:

"Now I'm thinking you've been run over by that bullet train or abducted by aliens. Please call as soon as you get this message. I don't care what time it is."

Richard might have smiled at the content of her last message if not for the obvious concern in Helen's voice. Instead, he suffered the guilt of knowing he hadn't thought to check in with her at all through the day. He glanced at the glowing numbers on the alarm clock and mentally calculated the time difference. It was 8 a.m. in Chicago, which meant he would be able to catch Helen at the office.

"I'm glad to hear you're not dead." It was the first thing she said when she realized he was on the line.

"I'm sorry you were concerned—I was out all day and just got your messages."

"I was only concerned because I've never known you to turn your cell phone off." She didn't sound annoyed so much as puzzled by the fact.

"I had to turn it off for *cha-no-yu,*" he said, a little defensively. "And then I forgot to turn it back on."

There was a long silence before Helen responded. "You...forgot?"

Richard couldn't blame her for sounding incredulous. He'd been shocked himself when he'd unclipped the phone and realized he'd never powered it back up after he left the teahouse with Jenny.

"You must have been quite...distracted."

This time there was amusement rather than surprise in her tone.

"I do have a lot on my mind getting ready for this merger."

She laughed. It was a sound he hadn't heard in a long time—since George's death and the disclosure of the company's precarious financial situation, no one at Hanson Media had much reason to laugh. He was happy to hear her doing so, even if her enjoyment came at his expense.

"You were ready long before you ever stepped on the plane," Helen reminded him.

"There's always more prep work that can be done in a situation such as this."

"That's true." Then she asked, "Who is she?"

"Who is who?"

She laughed again. "The woman you spent the day with."

"You're relentless, Helen."

"One of my finer attributes," she agreed. "Are you going to tell me about her?"

He knew she would continue to badger him until he did. "She's an American journalist who lives and works in Tokyo."

"And she's been showing you around," Helen guessed.

"Reluctantly."

"I can't imagine any woman would be reluctant to spend time with you."

Richard smiled wryly. "You haven't met Jenny."

"Am I going to?" Helen was evidently delighted by the possibility.

"I don't think so."

"Why not?"

"Because I have a job to do here and so does she."

"As long as the business is taken care of, no one would object to you mixing a little pleasure with it. And there isn't much you can do with respect to the merger right now, anyway."

"Unfortunately not," he agreed.

"When are you seeing her again?"

"What makes you think I am?"

"The fact that you didn't come out and say you weren't."

He shook his head. "I assume there was a reason you left so many messages on my voice mail other than to inquire how I'm spending my free time."

"I really just wanted to touch base," she admitted. "You know I get antsy when things are out of my control."

"Then maybe you should have come to Tokyo instead of me."

"With so much going on with Jack and Evan and Andrew, I thought it more important to keep an eye on things here. And I know you're more than capable of handling the negotiations."

"I appreciate your confidence," he said. "When are you coming?"

"You know me so well." He heard the smile in her voice.

"Then you have booked your flight?"

"I'll be there next Saturday."

Chapter Five

Jenny arrived at Richard's hotel the next morning without any definite plans. Since he'd been such a good sport through the tea ceremony and at the theater the day before, she decided to give him a few options. She suggested the Tokyo Tower, the Japanese Sword Museum or the East Garden of the Imperial Palace. His choice wasn't at all what she expected.

"Shopping?" Jenny echoed as she stepped into the revolving glass door to exit the hotel.

Richard smiled wryly as he followed her out into the sunshine. "It's not one of my favorite pastimes," he admitted. "But I need to pick up some gifts and souvenirs while I'm here, and I thought you could help me."

Gifts for his boss? Or a girlfriend back home? It shouldn't matter. If he wanted to shop for a dozen women, it wasn't any of her business. She wasn't going to start acting weird and proprietary just because he'd kissed her yesterday—even if it was a kiss that had made her mind numb and her toes curl.

"Was there anything in particular you're looking for?" she asked.

"Something for an eight-year-old girl and a five-year-old boy."

She turned south, toward the subway station, and asked casually. "Yours?"

"No." His response was quick and vehement. "Caitlin and Tyler are my niece and nephew."

"You mentioned yesterday that you'd been married, so I thought they might be your children."

He shook his head in emphatic denial. "No kids."

There were more questions she wanted to ask: How long were you married? Why did it end? Her curiosity wasn't motivated by personal interest but a simple desire to know what made a person make that kind of commitment—and then break it. Why would a man vow to love a woman forever, then walk away? Why would a mother give her away her child?

But it was evident from Richard's clipped tone that his marriage was a topic he didn't want to discuss, so she let it pass, reminding herself that his failed relationship was just one more reason not to get involved. The next time she opened her heart, she was determined that it would be to a man who could make a promise to her—and keep it. Her only obligation with respect to Richard Warren was to show him around Tokyo.

"If you want a uniquely Japanese shopping experience, there's no place better than Ginza," she told him.

Richard had never been anywhere like Ginza.

As they wandered through the shopping district, Jenny

pointed out famous department stores beside tiny shops selling traditional handmade crafts tucked next to galleries and ultra-modern showrooms. She dragged him from one store to the next, showing him the wares, explaining the history or tradition behind different items.

"You like to shop," he commented, noting the pink flush in her cheeks, the sparkle in her eyes, as she led him through yet another store.

Her smile was easy. "It's a definite vice."

"But is it your only vice?" he teased.

"The only one you need to worry about right now," she said.

"Well, I'm grateful for your help." Following her suggestions and guidance, he'd finished most of his shopping. For his nephew he'd picked up a kite shaped like a carp, which Jenny told him was a symbol of courage and strength and a traditional gift for young boys; for his brother and sister-in-law he'd found a ceramic Murasaki sake set; and for his mother he'd purchased a framed watercolor of Mount Fuji. "But I still don't have anything for Caitlin."

"You will." She took his arm to steer him down a small alley, then over a broken step and through a narrow doorway.

It was a doll shop. A tiny room with floor-to-ceiling shelves lined with white-faced dolls dressed in silk kimonos. He glanced around at the hundreds—maybe even thousands—of dolls, before selecting one at random for a closer examination.

"The workmanship and detail are amazing."

"It's an oyster shell doll. I had one when I was a little girl. My mom bought it for me on our first trip to Japan." She smiled. "I carted that doll everywhere with me until it finally got lost somewhere in our travels."

It was more information than she'd ever volunteered about herself, and he was eager to hear more. Maybe learning about the child she'd been would give him some insight into the woman she'd become. But he knew better than to pry—anytime he asked direct questions, she seemed to shut down.

"I cried when I realized it was gone," she admitted. "But I was almost a teenager by then—too old to be playing with dolls."

She shook her head, as if to shake off the memory, and smiled again. "But eight is just the right age for a gift like this. Still young enough to want to play with it, and old enough to know to take care of it."

"I think you're right," he agreed. "The only problem now is choosing the right one."

Jenny picked up another doll, stroked a hand gently over the hair. "This is like the one I had," she told him. "I still remember the glossy red lips and matching scarlet kimono."

"Then that's the one I'll get," he decided.

After his shopping was done, she took him to the Nissan gallery where he admired the latest offerings from the motor vehicle company, then to the Sony showroom where he played with the latest electronic gadgets.

"My mother always said that the only difference between men and boys was the price of their toys," she told him as they walked out of the store.

He smiled. "I imagine there's some truth in that."

"The truth is in the bag in your hand."

"It's a digital camera barely bigger than a credit card. How could anyone resist that?"

"I can't possibly imagine," she said, tongue in cheek.

He wouldn't give her the satisfaction of knowing that it

had been an impulse buy. He refused to admit that he rarely bothered to take pictures. Instead, he took it out of the box and snapped a quick photo of her.

He checked the display screen, pleased with the image he'd captured. He found the tantalizing glimpses of the woman beneath the surface even more captivating than her beauty, and there was just a hint of that woman in the picture he'd impulsively taken. There was the illusion of a smile tugging at the corners of her mouth and a glint of amusement in her deep green eyes. She intrigued him more than he wanted to admit, enticed him as no other woman had done in a very long time.

He tucked the camera into his pocket, wishing he could so easily tuck away his thoughts about Jenny, and fell into step with her again. They wandered some more, around the Gallery Center Building to look at the art, then through Hankyu and Seibu department stores.

Despite the sexual tension, which had been exacerbated rather than alleviated by the fiery kiss they'd shared the day before, Richard found it surprisingly easy to talk to her. But he noticed that while she was knowledgeable about any number of topics, she didn't offer a lot in the way of personal information. The revelation in the doll shop was the only real insight he'd been given, and he wanted to know so much more.

"Tell me about the story you wanted to write," he said, hoping—despite her loss of the assignment—that it wasn't a topic that would create new barriers.

"I pitched it to my editor as a piece about gender inequality in the contemporary workplace. As I began to research it, however, it became a story about sexual harassment with a prominent corporate VP at its center."

"No wonder you were annoyed when you lost the assignment."

She nodded. "I'd talked to five women—all of whom were either promised promotions if they provided sexual services to the boss or threatened with demotions if they refused to do so."

"None of these women ever complained?"

"He's a powerful and influential man—they didn't see any point."

"How did you get them to talk to you?"

"One of the women is a friend of mine," she admitted. "When she confided in me about what had happened, I guessed she wasn't the first victim. I suggested she approach some other women at work, and they agreed to talk to me, too. They believed that exposing his actions in a public forum—such as the newspaper—would help them get justice."

"How did your friend feel when she found out you weren't going to write the story?"

"She wasn't happy," Jenny admitted. "Especially when my replacement went to the boss to hear his response to the allegations."

"I'm really sorry, Jenny."

She shrugged. "There will be other stories."

"But you weren't just upset because you lost your byline, were you? You were upset because you'd let your friend down."

She was surprised that he'd so readily understood. Maybe, she reluctantly acknowledged, she'd been a little hasty in her judgment of him.

"Tell me about your job—why you wanted to be a

lawyer." She smiled. "Because I'm sure you didn't do so just to please your mother."

Richard didn't smile back. In fact, she thought she saw a shadow pass over his face, but it was gone so quickly she decided she'd imagined it.

"I went to law school because I like to argue," he told her. "And it seemed a good way to get paid for doing something I enjoy."

"That sounds like an oversimplified explanation," she complained.

"What do you want me to say—that I felt a burning need to uphold truth, justice and the American way?"

"Only if it's true."

"The truth is, my parents owned a coffee shop. My dad did the baking and tended the shop while my mother took care of my brother and me. They worked hard to make life easier for us, and I wanted to do something that I thought would make my parents proud."

"I'm sure you succeeded."

"Not entirely. My mother wanted me to become a district attorney."

"Why?"

She was sure she saw the shadow this time, but he only shrugged.

"Instead you chose to wage your legal battles over contract addendums and penalty clauses."

"Pretty much," he agreed.

"What about your wife? What kind of law did she practice?"

"What makes you think she's an attorney?"

"I have friends who are lawyers," she explained. "And

they all seem to be married to one another, having babies who will grow up to be the next generation of lawyers."

He smiled. "I guess there is a fair amount of inbreeding within the profession. And Marilyn—my ex-wife—is also a corporate attorney."

"It seems with so much in common, you'd have the foundation for a good marriage," Jenny noted.

"We thought so," he agreed. "We got married right out of law school, both of us young and ambitious. Six months later, she was offered a great job at a firm in Decatur. She decided to take it, and though we tried to make it work, time and distance eroded our relationship until there was nothing left."

"I don't imagine it was as easy to let go as you imply."

His mouth twisted into something that might have been a smile. "She made it easy when she decided to sleep with her new boss."

"Ouch." Again, she knew his explanation had only skimmed the surface and though she wanted to know more, she was reluctant to pursue what was obviously a painful topic for him. Instead, she glanced at her watch. "I had no idea it was getting to be so late."

"Do you have somewhere you have to be?" he asked.

"Actually, yes," she said. "And if we don't hurry, we're going to miss the first pitch."

The crowd was thick around the amusement park and outside the Tokyo Dome, so Jenny took Richard's hand to ensure they didn't get separated. She ignored the now-familiar tingle that skated through her veins when their fingers linked together. It didn't matter how his touch made her heart race and her heart pound—she was going to be smart and keep their relationship simple.

She led him through the gate, handing their tickets to the attendant. "It's not the White Sox or the Cubs," she told him. "But I thought it might be something you'd enjoy."

"She's smart and beautiful and she likes baseball— that's an almost irresistible combination."

"Only almost?" she teased, refusing to take his words seriously. "Wait until you see our seats."

She led him down section A16, four rows back from the infield, directly facing first base. Close enough to smell the dirt and sweat and feel the tension and excitement as the players stood along the baseline for the national anthem. When the last notes faded away, Jenny sat down beside Richard and breathed deeply to inhale the unique ambience of the ballpark.

"Those are the Yomiuri Giants," she told him, pointing to the home team in the white-and-orange uniforms. "They're the oldest and the most popular professional baseball team around, and they've won more pennants and series titles than any other team in Japan."

"Tokyo's version of the Yankees."

She nodded. "Tonight the Giants are playing against the Hanshin Tigers."

There was a collective cheer as the first pitch was thrown and a strike was called.

"Do you come to the games very often?" he asked.

"At least a few times a year. Samara likes to come with me sometimes."

"Your roommate is a baseball fan, too?"

"She doesn't understand much about the logistics of the game," Jenny confided. "But she appreciates a nicely toned butt in tight pants."

The next pitch was swung on and missed, and the crowd cheered again.

"What's the attraction for you?" Richard asked.

She answered without hesitation. "The crack of the bat when a fastball hits the sweet spot, a diving catch from center field, a well-turned double play, a full-count pitch in the bottom of the ninth of a tie game." Then she smiled. "And nicely toned butts in tight pants."

He shook his head. "I thought you were immune to that sort of thing."

"It's like shopping for a car. I can look without wanting to test drive."

The batter connected with the third pitch—a line-drive straight to the third baseman that was easily snagged for the first out. The fielders tossed the ball around as they waited for the next batter to step up to the plate, and Richard turned his attention to Jenny. "Who do you have to know to get seats like this?"

"It's not the 'who' so much as the 'what'," she admitted. "For these tickets, I had to endure endless hours of tedium and boredom."

The next batter swung at the first pitch, sending the ball deep into the foul territory of right field.

"The shareholder meeting," she explained in response to his quizzical look. "When my parents gave me their proxies, I negotiated for these along with them."

"These are your parents' seats?"

She nodded as the first ball was called, low and outside. "Although, between their business and travel, they don't get to come to many games."

"You said Samara sometimes comes with you—who else do you bring here?"

"Any one of a dozen different men," she lied glibly. She had no intention of admitting that when Samara wasn't available, it was usually her brother who came or, less frequently, a coworker she knew would enjoy the game.

"A dozen?"

"Usually only one at a time."

Ball two, low and outside again.

He slid an arm across the back of her chair.

She eyed him warily.

"And of the dozen men you've brought here, how many went home with you?"

"None—" another swing, another hit, this one into the right fielder's glove for the second out "—of your business."

"Yasushi told me you don't date. Why is that?"

She frowned. "You talked to Yasushi about me?"

"I was curious," he said easily, brushing his fingertips over her shoulder.

It was a casually intimate touch that made her skin burn and her heart pound.

"Now I'm curious about what he'd say if I told him you brought me to a Giants game."

She didn't need to look at him to know he was smiling.

"It doesn't matter because this isn't a date," she said firmly.

"Why aren't you dating anyone right now?"

"Why does there have to be a reason?"

"There doesn't have to be," he allowed. "But there usually is."

"Okay," she relented. "I ended a long-term relationship before I came back to Tokyo a few months ago."

"How long-term?"

"Two and a half years."

"That's longer than my marriage lasted," he admitted.

Jenny considered this revelation as she refocused her attention on the field, surprised to see that the Giants were leaving the field for their turn at bat. And annoyed to realize that she'd been so disconcerted by his casual touch, she'd completely missed the third out.

Richard enjoyed watching the game—at least after he got used to the incessant chanting of the crowd and the unusual background music. Japanese baseball fans might not be as loud as their American counterparts, but no one could claim they were any less enthusiastic.

But even more than the game, he enjoyed watching Jenny. The way her eyes would light up for a well-hit ball or darken with frustration over what she perceived to be an inaccurate call by the umpire, the enthusiasm with which she joined in the cheering, the simple enjoyment she showed in munching down on a hot dog generously slathered with mustard.

He would never have guessed she was a baseball fan. The woman he'd met outside of the TAKA boardroom had caught his eye because she was attractive. In the time they'd spent together since then, he'd realized there was a lot more to her than a pretty package. She was smart, passionate, fun and she didn't interrupt the game to ask about the infield fly rule. She was, quite possibly, the perfect woman.

The perfect woman for someone else, of course, because Richard wasn't in the market for a woman—perfect or otherwise. He was only killing time until Mr. Tetsugoro returned to Tokyo and the negotiations for the Hanson-TAKA merger finally commenced.

* * *

The Giants trounced the Tigers and they did so quickly. As Jenny and Richard filed out of the park with the rest of the crowd, she noted that it wasn't even nine o'clock. She considered suggesting a bar or nightclub, but she really just wanted to get home. As much as she'd enjoyed the day with Richard, she still wasn't completely comfortable with him.

It was the attraction, she knew, that kept getting in the way of what might have developed into a genuine friendship between them. Every time she started to relax, something would happen to remind her of the kiss they'd already shared and the desire that continued to simmer between them. A glance, a smile, a touch—any and all of these silent communications kept her on edge.

She wasn't afraid of him. Although she hadn't known him for very long and certainly didn't know him well, she trusted that he would respect the boundaries she'd set. She was afraid of her own response to him, of the longing that had started to stir deep inside her.

It would be smart to take a step back—several steps even. Because they'd both been honest about what they wanted and while she wasn't interested in a temporary affair, he couldn't offer her anything more.

But he did offer to see her home again. Insisted on it, in fact, and while Jenny tried to object, she was secretly pleased by the courtesy.

When they got to her apartment, he dug into one of the bags he carried to offer her a tissue-wrapped package. "This is for you."

She was surprised, pleased and curious all at the same time, with just a hint of caution dancing around the outside of her other emotions. She couldn't remember the last time anyone had spontaneously given her a gift. Brad certainly hadn't been the type to pick up little trinkets, and flowers had arrived for her only once each year—on Valentine's Day.

"Why?" she couldn't help but ask.

He smiled, as if he'd anticipated the question. "It's both a thank you and a bribe—in appreciation for a wonderful day and to entice you to spend tomorrow with me, too."

"I don't seem to have any other plans," she said.

"Don't you want to open it before you make any promises?"

She tore the paper away, curiosity overcome by stunned pleasure as she unwrapped the oyster shell doll. "But this was for your niece."

He shook his head. "I bought a purple one for Caitlin, because it's her favorite color. This one is for you."

Jenny stroked a hand over the doll's silky hair, her eyes misting with unexpected tears.

"It's beautiful. Thank you." She impulsively rose on her toes and touched her lips to his cheek.

It was intended as an expression of gratitude—an innocent kiss. But the heated awareness that suddenly sparked between them was anything but innocent. She stepped back to find his eyes on her, his gaze dark and intense.

The silence seemed to stretch between them for a long minute before he finally said, "You just broke one of your own rules."

She could only nod, her heart pounding so loudly he couldn't possibly be unaware of it.

"Not that I'm complaining." Richard traced the curve of her bottom lip with his fingertip once, then again. "I was just wondering if it meant that you're ready to throw all of the rules away."

She was tempted, oh so tempted, but definitely not ready.

"I can't." She clutched the doll against her chest and took a careful step back. "I'm sorry."

His smile was wry. "So am I. More than you can imagine."

Chapter Six

Jenny awoke in a rare mood Saturday morning—a fact that was immediately recognized by her roommate.

"Rough night?" Samara asked, spreading jam on a slice of toast.

"No," she responded as she made her way to the coffee pot. She had no intention of admitting that she'd dreamed of Richard last night—of kissing him, touching him, making love with him. A dream inspired by too vivid memories of the kiss they'd shared two days earlier.

It was just a kiss, she reminded herself. Nothing to get all worked up about. Except that it had been *just* a kiss, and that was *exactly* what had her all worked up. She wanted more.

And her imagination was far too creative in supplying the details of exactly what and how much more. She swallowed a mouthful of coffee, needing the jolt of caffeine to shake off the last remnants of the dream and plant her firmly back into reality.

"If it's any consolation," Samara said, "Richard was on his way out last night as I was coming in, and he looked just as frustrated as you do now."

"I'm not frustrated," she denied. "I'm annoyed."

"Oh?"

"It's Saturday and I wanted nothing more than to sleep late and laze around the apartment all day. Instead, I'm on tour guide duty. *Again.*"

"You never sleep late," Samara pointed out.

"I never get the chance."

Samara nibbled on her toast. "I think you need to sleep with Richard."

It was the casual delivery that surprised Jenny even more than the words. She choked on her coffee, sputtered. "What kind of a statement is that?"

Her friend shrugged. "Obviously something has to happen to elevate your sexual tension."

"Alleviate," she corrected automatically. "And I'm not tense."

"Liar."

She refilled her mug with coffee. "Even if I was tense, sleeping with Richard Warren wouldn't help. I have no interest in yet another dead-end relationship."

"Who said anything about a relationship? I was talking about a fling."

Jenny shook her head. "You know I'm not good at remaining emotionally detached."

"And you're falling for him already," Samara guessed.

She shook her head again. She wasn't entirely sure how she felt about Richard, but she was confident she wasn't falling for him. She enjoyed being with him, talking to him, even arguing with him. And each hour she spent with him tempted her to disregard her common sense and open up her heart again, but that was something she wouldn't do. His presence in her life was only temporary and his interest in her would decrease in direct proportion to the increased demands of his job. As soon as he was able to get back to the bargaining table, he would forget about her. She'd be a fool to think otherwise.

And Jenny wasn't going to be a fool again.

They started the morning with a quick tour through the Tsukiji Market then moved on to the Tokyo Tower and the Japanese Sword Museum. It seemed to Richard that Jenny wanted to ensure he saw absolutely everything Tokyo had to offer and was focused resolutely on the task.

She was also, Richard noted, as tightly wound as the spool of string on the kite he'd bought for his nephew during yesterday's shopping excursion.

As she strode briskly down the corridor of the Metropolitan Art Museum, he reached out to touch her arm. She jolted at the contact.

"You startled me," she said.

"I just wanted to ask if you had signed up for some tourist version of *The Amazing Race* with me as your unwitting companion."

"Of course not." But her cheeks colored slightly. "There's so much still to see and you'll be back at work on Monday—"

Her words halted when he took her hand and linked their fingers. He saw her brows draw together, just the slightest hint of a scowl, and he imagined her agile mind rapidly sorting through possible responses to the overture, battling between annoyance and acceptance. If she tugged her hand away, it might place too much importance on a casual gesture. If she left her fingers entwined with his, it might suggest she didn't object to his touching her.

He wasn't surprised when she disentangled her hand from his.

"I just don't think there's anything to be learned by seeing Japan at warp speed."

"I didn't want you to miss anything."

"And I don't want to spend the whole day being dragged from one thing to the next because you think that's what I want."

"What do you want to do?" she asked warily.

"I want you to stop thinking like a tour guide and tell me what you'd most like to do on a day off."

"Sleep in and stay in my pajamas all day."

"It's already too late for the sleeping in part," he said, trying not to think about the second half of her statement. But his errant imagination was already sorting through the options. Skimpy satin, peekaboo lace, seductive silk. The possibilities were endlessly enticing and it took a determined effort to refocus his mind on the conversation. "And I don't believe you're the type to lounge in bed, anyway."

"I didn't know you had to be a certain *type* for that."

"You do," he told her. "And you're not it."

"How do you know?"

"Too much energy and ambition."

She frowned.

"It wasn't a criticism—just an observation."

"You don't know me well enough to leap to a conclusion like that," she said, just a little defensively.

"After spending the better part of three days together, I think I can hazard a few guesses. And I'd know you even better if you'd stop pushing me away."

"I'm here with you now, aren't I?"

"Are you? Because I feel like I'm being shuttled around by Jennifer Anderson, professional ambassador of Japan, rather than the warm, friendly woman who cheered beside me at the baseball game last night."

She wrinkled her nose. "No one calls me Jennifer."

"And that," he said, "is one of the few pieces of personal information you've voluntarily imparted."

"You asked for someone to show you the sights. That's what I've been doing."

"I wanted *you* to show me around because I wanted to spend time with you. Not the reporter or the tour guide, but the real woman. I wanted a chance to know you—your likes and dislikes, your hopes and dreams."

"I'm not as complicated as you seem to think."

He wondered what she was hiding, what she was afraid of. But he knew she'd only withdraw further if he pushed for answers to the questions that lingered in his mind. So he only said, "We can start with how you would spend your free time on a Saturday afternoon." Then he smiled. "We'll work our way up to what kind of pajamas you wear later on."

"A picnic," she said, pointedly ignoring his comment.

"You mean lunch on a blanket on the grass?"

"That's exactly what I mean." She led the way through the exit and into the bright sunshine outside. "It's a beautiful day and I know the perfect place for it."

He tried to remember if he'd ever been on a picnic. He didn't think so. He did business lunches and negotiated contracts over cocktails—dining on the ground in the great outdoors was far outside his area of expertise.

"What's for lunch?" he asked suspiciously.

She already had her cell phone out and was punching in numbers. "We'll pick something up."

Before he could question her about the "something," she was talking in Japanese to whoever was on the other end of the line. After a brief conversation, of which he failed to understand a single word other than her name, she tucked her phone away.

"I had no idea you were so fluent in the language."

She grinned. "It might sound like I am, but I still make the occasional mistake when I'm translating words in my mind. Instead of salad and sandwiches, we might be eating grilled eels marinated in sake."

"*You* might be eating grilled eels," he said. "I'm really not that hungry."

She laughed and tucked her arm through his.

It was a casual and friendly gesture, completely within the boundaries she'd established for their relationship, and yet he felt a jolt of desire, hard and fast, when her breast inadvertently brushed against him.

As they exited the museum, she tilted her head to look at him. "And if you really need to know—I wear flannel."

He sighed with exaggerated disappointment. "You could have at least let me have my fantasies."

She laughed again. "I'll let you share my lunch instead."

Jenny hoped to get in and out of the hotel without anyone but the kitchen staff ever knowing she'd been there, unprepared to face an interrogation from her brother if he saw her with Richard. John Anderson had always been protective of his little sister, but he'd been even more so since her recent return to Tokyo after yet another failed relationship.

It was the newspaper that thwarted her plans.

The headline of the front page caught her attention as she moved past the seating area in the center of the lobby.

"What is it?" Richard asked.

She picked up the paper. "Jiro Mikodashi was fired yesterday."

He looked at her blankly.

"The VP at Kakubishi," she explained. "My sexual harassment story was apparently scooped by the *Herald*."

"I thought your editor had reassigned it."

She nodded. "Unfortunately, Cameron Parks completely missed the point of it. His report on allegations of sexual harassment in the workplace was buried on page twenty of yesterday's paper because it gave no mention of the VP. But the victims must have decided to fight back." Her lips curved. "My editor isn't going to be happy."

"Then why are you smiling?"

"Because I'm hopeful that next time he'll think twice about reassigning a story I've researched." She dropped the paper back onto the table.

"Does that mean you're not still mad at me?" Richard asked.

"It means I've resigned myself to being stuck in the society pages for a while longer. You were really just a convenient target for my frustration this time around."

"This time?" he echoed. "Has this happened before?"

"Twice in the past six months," she admitted.

"Why do you put up with it?"

"Because I don't have a lot of recourse," she admitted.

"Despite my experience at the *New York Times,* I'm one of the youngest reporters on staff here."

"It must make you wonder if coming to Tokyo was a smart career decision."

"It wasn't a career decision at all but a personal one."

"Because of your family?" he guessed.

She felt torn between pleasure and apprehension as she saw her brother making his way across the marble tile of the lobby toward them. "Because of my family," she agreed.

"I heard a rumor you were here," John said when he drew nearer.

She smiled. "Didn't Mom tell us not to listen to rumors?"

"It's not really a rumor if it's true." He bent to kiss her cheek. "You weren't going to sneak out without saying hi, were you?"

"I was trying." But she softened the admission with another smile. "You know I don't like interrupting when you're busy."

"And you know I'm never too busy for you." His cool blue-eyed gaze shifted to fix on Richard. "Or to meet your friends."

Obviously that was a request for an introduction. "John, meet Richard Warren. Richard, this is my brother, Jonathon."

As the two men shook hands, Jenny could almost see the questions flipping through her brother's mind as if they were on cue cards.

"Richard is a lawyer from Chicago working on the Hanson-TAKA merger," Jenny told her brother, preempting what she guessed would be his first inquiry.

That information earned a slight nod. "Room 2212."

"Yes." Richard seemed surprised that the hotel manager would know such a detail; Jenny wasn't.

"Mori Taka keeps one of the penthouse suites reserved

for his personal use," she explained. "And TAKA guests always stay at this hotel."

"I can see why," Richard said. "My rooms are spectacular."

"Has the service been satisfactory?" her brother asked. He nodded.

"I'm sure Mr. Warren will complete a guest survey card when he checks out," Jenny said.

The corners of John's mouth tipped up a fraction, an acknowledgment he'd got the hint although not a guarantee he would heed her warning. "In the meantime," he said smoothly, "why don't you both join me for lunch in the dining room?"

She shook her head. "We can't. And to clarify, Richard is a business associate and Mr. Taka asked me to show him around Tokyo."

"I didn't ask," John said.

"But you were wondering."

"You're my little sister." He was speaking to her but his gaze was on Richard again as he said, "It's my job to look out for you."

"It's your job to look after this hotel," she reminded him. "I can take care of myself."

"Meiji Jingu is the Shinto shrine dedicated to the souls of Emperor Meiji and Empress Shoken," Jenny told Richard as they passed under the massive wooden torii that gated the entrance to the park. "The grounds of the shrine are covered by a forest of more than a hundred thousand trees donated by people from all over Japan."

He walked beside her along the wide gravel path, conscious of the city sounds fading away as they made their way deeper into the park. "I wouldn't have imagined there was anything like this here," he admitted. "When they show images of Tokyo on the news or in movies—it's always the towering buildings and glittering neon."

"Every city needs somewhere like this," Jenny told him. "A refuge from the frantic pace of urban society."

"And yet you seem to fit as easily into that world as you do into this one."

She shrugged. "When you live in ten different countries before the age of ten, you learn to adapt."

"Not everyone would," he disagreed. "Did you enjoy traveling so much?"

"Most of the time. Then we moved to Tokyo when my brother started high school. My parents wanted him—wanted both of us," she amended, "to be settled and able to concentrate on our studies. It was the first time we'd really had a chance to make friends. But still, as soon as there was a vacation—or even a long weekend—we'd be off to somewhere else again."

"Is that why your brother's so protective of you—because you spent so much time together as kids?"

She smiled as she led him off the path and onto a grassy area partially shaded by nearby trees. "John's a little over-protective, which I have a tendency to rebel against."

"Is that why you don't work at the hotel?"

"I don't work at the hotel because I'm not diplomatic enough to succeed in the hospitality industry." She took a blanket out of the basket he carried and spread it on the grass.

"I imagine there are plenty of positions that wouldn't require you to interact with the guests," he said, helping to straighten a corner.

"True, so maybe my decision was partly based on a

need to be independent—to end the comparisons." She winced. "I didn't mean to actually say that out loud."

"Whose comparisons?" he asked gently.

She knelt and began unpacking the picnic basket. "My own," she admitted. "Ever since we were little, I've tried to be as good as John at something. But he was always older, stronger, faster, smarter. And he'd always wanted to be part of the hotel business, so it made sense for me to find something else, something that was uniquely my own."

"Are you happy with what you're doing?"

"I am. I don't have any desire to be an investigative reporter who gets sent off to some distant country torn apart by war or devastated by natural disaster every time the newswire hums.

"I want to report news that is more relevant and substantial than what I write now for the society pages," she admitted. "But I also want a home and a family, and I want to go home to them every night. I won't ever let it take precedence over my children."

"Is that what you feel your parents did?"

"No," she responded immediately, maybe a little guiltily. "I didn't mean to give the impression that John and I were neglected, because we weren't. There were always nannies and tutors and play dates to keep us busy and out of trouble. But there were occasions when I wished my mom and dad had been around more."

She shook her head. "That sounds incredibly selfish. They gave us every opportunity any child could want, and yet, there were times when all I wanted was to stay in one place."

"It doesn't sound selfish." He took the wine and corkscrew she passed to him and started to open the bottle. "It just sounds like a child who was shuffled around a lot."

Her smile was wistful. "I used to wonder how my life would be different if..."

"If what?"

There was another pause—maybe a hesitation—as she poured the Bordeaux into two crystal glasses, then she shrugged again. "If things had been different. If I'd had parents who were settled in one place."

He wondered what she'd really been thinking, what had caused the hint of sadness in the depths of her eyes. Because he knew her thoughts weren't as simple as her response implied.

He sipped his wine as he debated whether to advance or retreat. He wanted her—the more time he spent with her, the more certain he was of that simple fact. And it didn't seem to matter how different they were or how many reasons they each had for not wanting to get involved. Except he realized he didn't really know her reasons.

"Tell me about him."

"Who?" she asked warily.

"Your ex-boyfriend. The one you left before you came back to Tokyo," he said. "I'm assuming he's the reason you're determined to keep me at a distance."

Jenny picked up her glass, set it back down again without drinking. She didn't need alcohol clouding her judgment when his mere proximity seemed to do that so effectively.

"You said you broke up with him about six months ago."

She nodded. Six months, two weeks and five days.

That was how long it had been since she'd left Brad in New York, but it had been longer than that since she'd had sex. And it was sexual deprivation, pure and simple, that was responsible for the power of the attraction she felt for Richard Warren.

"What happened?"

She shrugged, deliberately casual. "I wanted more than he was willing to give me."

"A commitment?" he guessed.

"That's usually what scares a man off, isn't it? And though I'm not denying that I want to get married and have a family of my own someday, all I wanted from Brad was to be a priority in his life."

"That's what he ran away from?"

She managed a smile. "Brad was always running toward the next big headline rather than away from anything else."

"He was an idiot."

"I like to think so." She selected a sandwich but set it down on her plate without taking a bite. "What's your story?"

"What makes you think I have one?"

"Everyone has a story."

"Not necessarily an interesting one."

Obviously he still wasn't going to tell her about his failed marriage. "Okay," she said. "Tell me about the scar on your chin. How'd you get it?"

He rubbed his finger over the spot and smiled. "Making cinnamon buns."

He poured more wine into both of their glasses, giving no indication that he intended to expand on his response.

"You're going to have to explain that," she told him.

"I was five—maybe six years old," he told her. "I always liked being with my dad in the kitchen, but I especially liked the smell of cinnamon buns baking, and he would sometimes let me help make them. One day I was standing on chair beside the counter, helping spread the cinnamon and sugar mixture onto the rolled out dough and I leaned too far, tipped the chair and smacked my chin on the counter."

She winced with instinctive sympathy. "I bet that hurt."

He shrugged. "I don't really remember, but I do remember hearing about it. Mr. Tortelli—a retired judge who lived in the neighborhood and one of my father's most regular and loyal customers tell the story in very dramatic fashion—of The Day Of No Cinnamon Buns At Warren's Café."

She listened, mesmerized by the nostalgia that warmed his voice. Despite the incident, it was obviously a happy time in his childhood.

"Apparently my father was more concerned about the blood than the baking, and he forgot to take the first batch out of the oven before he took me to the hospital. And the second batch, which I had been helping with, had to be thrown out because I'd bled all over the counter.

"I got three stitches and Mr. Tortelli got a tale of woe to share over his morning coffee for the next twenty years or so."

"He doesn't sound like a very nice man," she said, automatically defensive of the child Richard had been.

"Mr. Tortelli was a fabulous character," he explained. "He came in every morning for his coffee and a sweet roll and to grumble about me being underfoot. He'd talk to anyone who would listen about the one time he had to have an apple Danish instead his customary cinnamon bun because I didn't have the sense to keep both my feet on solid ground.

"Mr. Tortelli never had any kids of his own and he liked to claim he never wanted any. But he carried candies in his pocket—the crunchy mint ones with the soft chocolate centers—and he always managed to slip one to each of me and my brother along with a few coins before he grumbled his way out the door again." Richard smiled again.

"My father often said that Mr. Tortelli was the reason

he got up at 3:00 a.m. every morning to bake. He told me that it didn't matter what I chose to do with my life so long as I was there for the people who counted on me to do my job."

"You're close to your dad, aren't you?" she asked gently. "I can hear it in your voice when you talk about him."

He nodded. "I was."

"Was?" She frowned. "What happened?"

The happy memories that had warmed his smile and his voice were gone, replaced by stark emptiness and raw pain. "He was murdered."

Chapter Seven

Jenny immediately regretted her prying. She was always curious about family dynamics—at least with respect to *other* people's families—but she wished now she'd never asked the question.

Richard's gaze was focused on something over her shoulder, or maybe somewhere in another time, and though his words might have been matter-of-fact, she heard the anguish in his tone. She lived with an emptiness deep inside herself from never having known her birth mother. She couldn't begin to imagine the horrible void that had been left inside Richard when his father-a man he'd known and loved—was abruptly and violently taken away.

"It was summer vacation after my first year of law school," he said. "My father was so proud of me—the first Warren to go to college, and on a scholarship.

"Anyway, it was a hot night and he was closing up when a teenage junkie—a skinny fifteen-year-old girl hopped up on some kind of drugs and looking to score some more—came into the café waving a gun around and demanding money. My dad gave her the cash in the register, but he'd already sent me out to make the night deposit so there was only about fifty dollars that he'd kept for the start of business the next day."

He recited the facts evenly, almost dispassionately, but she heard the bleakness in his voice.

"She was furious and still strung out enough to be dangerous. And she put the gun to my father's head and pulled the trigger."

She touched his hand, not objecting when he turned his over to link their fingers together. "I'm so sorry."

"He wasn't even fifty years old, and he'd always been healthy and strong. He was the cornerstone of our family, then suddenly he was gone."

"That must have been horrible." It was an inane and inadequate response, but the only thing she could think of to say in the moment.

He nodded. "It was a shock for all of us. Especially my mother. For months after, she went through the motions of living. Then his killer finally went to trial. My mom sat in the courtroom for the entire proceeding—six days of arguments and evidence and testimony.

"Unfortunately the only evidence the prosecution had was circumstantial. The gun, with the girl's fingerprints all over it, was excluded because it had been found during an illegal search. Without the weapon to tie her to the crime, she was acquitted."

She could only imagine the fury and frustration he must

have felt when the verdict was read in the courtroom. She squeezed his hand gently. "How did your family take it?"

"My mother was devastated all over again. All she'd wanted was justice for her husband. She harassed the D.A., demanding a new trial. She petitioned the courts. She became a crusader—determined to change the laws and the world. When she didn't succeed, she turned her attention to me."

"That's why she wanted you to become a criminal prosecutor," she realized.

He nodded. "I was in my final year of law school by that time and she wanted me to apply for a job with the district attorney's office or for a clerkship with the courts. It didn't matter to her that I had no interest in criminal law—and even less after my father was killed—she just wanted me to make a difference."

"I can understand that she would be angry and disillusioned with the system," Jenny admitted. "But I can't believe she expected you to make it your battle."

He shrugged. "I sent out a dozen applications, including one to the local D.A.'s office. It was a half-hearted measure to appease her.

"I never thought they would actually offer me a job. Maybe it was because of my father that they did. But I also got an offer from Shotwell Cunningham, one of the top ten firms in Chicago. The day I started work there was the same day my mother followed through on her threat to take my younger brother and move away to a little town called Crooked Oak. She said that if I wasn't willing to do my part, she needed to move somewhere she could feel safe.

"And maybe that was a factor in her decision," he allowed, "but she didn't have to move all the way to North Carolina."

"I can't imagine how awful that must have been for you. First losing your dad, then being manipulated by your mother and cut off from your brother."

"She thought I owed it to my father," he explained. "Because he'd made sacrifices so I could go the law school, she thought I had a responsibility to use that education to bring his killer to justice.

"I could see her point, but I couldn't let myself be drawn into her cause, to become part of what was tearing her apart. And she has never forgiven me for letting her down."

"I'm sure that's not true," she said, although the picture she was getting of his mother didn't make her certain of anything except that Mrs. Warren had treated her elder son unfairly.

His smile was bitter. "She didn't even come to my law school graduation."

Unfairly *and* horribly, she mentally amended, trying to imagine how he must have felt not to have such an important milestone acknowledged by his closest family. "I'm sorry, Richard."

"That was eight years ago," he said dismissively. "It hardly matters anymore."

"Of course it matters," she said. "The actions of a parent can have lasting impact on a child's life."

"I was hardly a child. In fact, it was only a few weeks after that Marilyn and I got married."

And she was starting to suspect that the estrangement from his family was a factor in his decision to marry so quickly. "Was your mother at the wedding?"

"I didn't invite her."

No doubt he hadn't done so because he didn't want to be hurt again when his mother declined to share in that special day. She recognized the self-preservation tactic because she'd used it herself. She'd left James because she'd known he wouldn't stay with her, then she'd followed the same pattern with both Kevin and Brad.

But understanding Richard's reasoning didn't blind her to the results. His action had hurt his mother and cemented their separation, and her heart went out to both the parent and child who still bore the scars of a tragedy.

"She sent a card and a gift," Richard continued. "Later, when I called to tell her that Marilyn and I were getting a divorce, she told me she'd known all along that the Crock-Pot she gave us would last longer than our marriage."

Jenny winced sympathetically. "That was harsh."

"She's always known how to make her point most effectively."

"Do you ever see her anymore?"

"Once, sometimes twice, a year. A few years ago I tried to make more frequent visits, as if doing so would somehow bridge the gap between us. But she still can't forgive me for my failure to right the wrong of my father's death."

"What about your brother? You carry photos of your niece and nephew in your wallet, you remember their birthdays—obviously you're close to them."

"Not as close as I'd like, but things are a lot better between us than they used to be. On top of my mother's negative attitude, Steven had his own reasons for resenting me."

"Such as?"

"The fact that I went to law school. After my father died, there just wasn't enough money for my brother to go to college."

"You said you had a scholarship."

"I did, but my parents still helped out with additional expenses. My brother didn't have that option. He was stuck.

Now that he has a successful business as a mechanic and a beautiful wife and two children who adore him, he's happy."

"It sounds as though you envy him," Jenny said.

"I used to," he admitted. "But after my divorce, I accepted that I couldn't have everything I wanted—that my career had to come first."

If Jenny needed any further reminder that he wasn't right for her, it was there in his own words. He might have opened up to her, sharing a lot of his personal history and past hurt, but he wasn't the man who could make her dreams of marriage and a family come true. No woman would ever take precedence over his career—and she had already lived enough of her life in second place.

Richard noticed that Jenny kept casting worried glances at the gray sky as they packed up the remnants of their picnic. It had been a beautiful sunny day when they first arrived, but the weather was changing quickly and rain seemed imminent.

"I don't suppose you have an umbrella in this basket?" he asked as they started to make their way out of the park.

"I wasn't supposed to need one," she said. "The forecast was for clear skies."

She hadn't finished speaking when the clouds opened up and fat drops of rain started to fall. "It was wrong," he told her.

She narrowed her eyes at him. "Obviously."

They quickened their pace, but Richard soon realized why she'd been so distressed by the unexpected precipitation. The blouse she was wearing was white and made of some very filmy fabric that was, within minutes, not just wet but very transparent. Her bra was also white and her nipples were beaded beneath the delicate lace.

Despite the moisture in the air, Richard's mouth was suddenly dry thinking that the young co-eds who participated in wet T-shirt contests during spring break had nothing on Jenny Anderson.

She crossed her arms over her chest. He didn't know if it was because she was cold or because she was aware of the transparency of her garment. He wished he had a jacket he could give her, but he'd opted not to wear one in the ninety degree heat. Then he remembered the blanket. He tugged it out of the picnic basket and draped it over her shoulders.

She turned, her expression reflecting both surprise and gratitude. "Thank you."

He smiled, forcing his gaze to remain on her face despite the urge to let it drop lower. "I can't have my tour guide catching a chill," he said lightly.

"What about the tourist?"

"I live in Chicago," he reminded her. "I'm made of tough stuff. Although I wouldn't object to a cup of coffee to take away the chill when we get back to your apartment."

"That sounds reasonable," she agreed.

Despite the rain, Jenny had enjoyed her day with Richard and found herself reluctant to let it end. As she clutched the ends of the blanket during the short subway ride to her apartment, she worried that she was beginning to enjoy his company too much.

She didn't delude herself into thinking there would be many more days like the last few they'd spent together. Richard's stay in Tokyo was limited. But even so, she knew she was starting to care about him. All it took was one kiss and a few casual touches. Or maybe it was the knowledge of everything he'd been through and his willingness to share it with her that made Jenny want to drop the shields around her heart.

What was wrong with her? Was she so desperately needy that she latched on to anyone who showed the slightest interest? Was she so scarred by her abandonment as a child that she couldn't be alone? She didn't want to think so, but she couldn't think of any other explanation for her inability to control her own feelings.

She hesitated on the sidewalk outside her apartment, suddenly aware that she'd never invited a man inside. As Samara liked to remind her, in the six months since she'd been back in Tokyo, she hadn't even been on a date. And maybe that was the reason for her hesitation—that inviting Richard into her apartment, showing him where she lived and sharing conversation would seem too much like a date.

Not that she wasn't ready to start dating again. Contrary to what Samara thought, Jenny was definitely over Brad and ready to get on with her life. But she wasn't going to date anyone who was the least bit similar to her ex. She was determined to finally break the cycle of dead-end relationships once and for all.

But she had offered him coffee and she wasn't going to renege on that promise. As she unlocked the exterior door, however, she made a point of saying, "Just because you're coming up to my apartment doesn't mean this is a date."

"Of course not," he agreed easily.

Too easily.

She eyed him warily and caught the twitch of his lips as he tried not to smile. She started to question him, then decided she didn't want to know and led the way up the narrow stairs to her fourth floor apartment.

Richard responded to her unspoken query, anyway. "It's not a date until I kiss you."

While Jenny was changing, Richard took advantage of her absence to survey the small living room. There was a sofa and one armchair, an end table, lamp, television. On the table there were thick candles that had burned halfway down set in a shallow bowl filled with decorative stones. The oatmeal sofa was dotted with colorful pillows in various shades of orange and red. It was small but tidy with all the little feminine touches noticeably lacking in his own apartment.

There was a trio of framed photographs on the table. He picked up the nearest one—a picture of Jenny and Samara both in caps and gowns—obviously their graduation day. He set the frame back down and selected another. This one was of Samara and her great-grandmother, and the resemblance between the two women was striking. The third photo was of Jenny and a couple he assumed were her parents. The man had dark hair and dark eyes and the woman was blond with blue eyes. Richard gazed closely at the trio but could discern no obvious familial resemblance among them. He found it strange that she didn't look like either of her parents or her brother, and yet she seemed so familiar to him.

Or maybe Jenny was right—maybe his subconscious was playing tricks on him, giving him a reason for his fixation on her rather than admit it was purely a physical attraction.

She came out of her bedroom dressed in a pair of faded

jeans and a soft yellow T-shirt that clung enticingly to her curves. She'd brushed her hair out so that it hung straight to her shoulders, and he noticed that the ends were still slightly damp.

She smiled at him, a little hesitantly, as if she was suddenly aware that they were alone in her apartment but not quite sure how they'd got there. "You said you wanted coffee?"

"That would be great," he agreed.

While she was making the coffee, he sat at the little table in the kitchen and watched her. After a few minutes, she joined him, leaning over to slide a mug across the table to him. As she did so, her hair fell forward.

He couldn't resist the opportunity, and he reached over to brush a wayward strand off her cheek and tuck it behind her ear. "Did you know that your hair looks like gold in the sun but now, slightly damp, it's more like copper?"

She pulled back slightly.

He smiled. "And when you're nervous, your eyes get dark—like bottomless pools."

She wrapped her hands around her mug. "Do you think a few words of poetic flattery will seduce me, Richard?"

He shook his head. "No, you'd appreciate straightforward honesty more than smooth dialogue."

"You'd be right," she admitted.

"That's why I'm telling you straight out that I want you in my bed."

She set her mug down too quickly, too hard, and coffee sloshed over the rim. She jumped up to get a dishcloth to wipe the spill. "I thought we agreed that wouldn't be smart."

"It's probably not smart," he said. "But I'm starting to think it's inevitable."

"It's not." She shook her head. "You might be content with casual relationships, but I'm looking for something more."

"I won't ever make you any promises I can't keep."

"I'm not asking for any promises. I'm only telling you why it won't happen."

"I guess we'll just have to wait and see about that."

She shook her head, but she was smiling. "You're being pushy again."

"Persistent," he corrected.

"We're completely mismatched."

"That doesn't seem to have diminished the chemistry between us."

"It's the whole opposites attract thing. Maybe we'd have great sex for a while, but it would fizzle soon enough."

"Couldn't we at least enjoy the great sex while it lasts?"

"I need more than short-term physical pleasure," she told him.

"Have you ever had a relationship based purely on physical pleasure?"

"No," she admitted.

He smiled. "Then don't knock it until you try it."

She shook her head. "That little gem of clichéd advice isn't going to make me throw away my long-term goals for the momentary pleasure of having sex with you."

His smile only widened. "It sounds as though you've given this some thought."

He could tell by the troubled expression on her face that she'd given it more thought than she was willing to admit. He wondered if she'd thought about it as often as he had. If the idea snuck up on her at the most inopportune times during the day, if it plagued her dreams at night.

"Only because Samara planted the idea in my mind," she said.

"Your roommate thinks you should sleep with me?"

"She thinks I'm still in love with my ex and sleeping with another man is a first necessary step to getting over him."

His smile turned into a frown. "I'm not interested in being part of your therapy."

"I don't need therapy," she said. "Because I'm not still hung up on Brad."

As much as Richard wanted to believe her, he was disturbed by the possibility that she was still carrying a torch for her ex. Although he was intrigued by the idea of tangling up the sheets with Jenny, he had too much pride to let himself be used as a substitute for another man. "Are you sure about that, Jenny?"

"My relationship with Brad ended more than six months ago—I'm sure."

He nodded. "Good. Now we can both be sure that when you end up in my bed, it will be because you want to be with me and no one else."

"Don't you mean *if?*" she challenged.

He smiled. "No."

Despite his earlier teasing and innuendo, Richard didn't kiss her goodbye.

He paused at the door for a moment, his gaze locked with hers. After a seemingly endless moment, his eyes dropped to her mouth, lingered.

She felt her breath catch in her throat, heard her heart pound in her ears. He lifted a hand, stroked his fingers softly and ever so slowly down her cheek, and said, "Good night, Jenny."

Then he was gone.

She hadn't realized she'd been holding her breath until she let it out after the door closed behind him.

It was a sigh of relief, of course. She was grateful that he was respecting the boundaries she'd established. But at the same time, she was frustrated and disappointed, too.

She turned to see Samara waving her hand in front of her face like a makeshift fan. "Is it hot in here or is it just me?"

"It's just you," Jenny told her.

Samara grinned. "I'm starting to think that Richard Warren is as smart as he is good-looking."

"Why would you think that?"

"Because he knows that if he came on too strong, you'd push him away. Instead, he's taking it slow, drawing you in."

"He's not drawing me anywhere," she denied.

"And he's doing it so cleverly you don't even realize it's happening."

Jenny picked up the remote, flicked on the television.

Her friend perched on the arm of the couch. "What are your plans with Mr. Warren for tomorrow?"

"I'm not seeing him tomorrow."

"Why not?"

"Because the negotiations for the merger are scheduled to resume on Monday and Richard needs to prepare."

Samara sank down beside her on the couch. "Okay, I guess this is where you can say I told you so."

But Jenny wasn't feeling smug, just miserable. Because as often as she'd reminded herself that Richard's interest in her was only temporary, she didn't want it to be true.

Richard stood at the window and looked out into the night at the wonderland of concrete and steel splashed with garish neon lights.

Maybe it was because he'd talked to Jenny about his family today that he found himself thinking about them tonight, wondering what his father would have thought about his son—the lawyer—in this fancy hotel suite in Japan. More than anything, Stan Warren had wanted his children to have an education, to have the opportunities of the world opened up to them. Opportunities he'd never had.

Richard's lips curved as he imagined his father surveying the same scene that was spread out before him now. Stan would have been more puzzled than impressed by Tokyo, although he would undoubtedly have been pleased by his son's success.

His father had once confessed to having had big dreams of his own—plans of going to college, building a career— but then he'd met and fallen in love with Richard's mother. Nancy had ended up pregnant before they'd graduated from high school, and Stan had married her without a second thought. And though she'd lost that baby a few weeks later, he'd known he didn't want to be without her.

Richard had asked him once if he'd ever regretted what he'd given up, the life he might have had. His father had answered without hesitation.

"Sometimes in life you make choices. Sometimes you make sacrifices. Falling in love isn't one of those times— it's not a choice and it's never a sacrifice. It's the greatest opportunity. And if the woman you love loves you back, it's the greatest gift."

His brief marriage had suggested a far different reality to Richard. And though he was certain his father would be proud of what he'd done with his career, he wasn't so sure he'd approve of the mess he'd made of the rest of his life.

Divorced from his wife, alienated from his mother, Richard was—aside from a few close friends—alone in the world.

Usually he took comfort in the fact that there was no one to answer to, no one depending on him. Tonight, it only made him feel lonely.

With a sigh that was both resigned and regretful, he turned away from the window and back to the laptop humming quietly on the antique desk. He sat down and stared at the screen, but he continued to be preoccupied by a certain green-eyed journalist who had the softest, most kissable lips he'd ever tasted.

He'd been with other women. More beautiful women, more experienced women. And yet none of them had ever haunted his thoughts the way that Jenny did.

What was he doing with her? It was a question he'd asked himself at least a dozen times. A question he still couldn't answer except to acknowledge, with more than a hint of regret, that he had no business pursuing her.

By her own admission, she didn't do casual relationships. And Richard didn't do anything else.

Jenny was in the middle of inputting a story for the next day's paper when Richard called her at work Monday afternoon. She hadn't expected to hear from him for at least a few days, knowing he would be immersed in meetings with the TAKA people, and she'd been prepared for the possibility that she might not hear from him at all.

"I was just thinking about you and wanted to hear your voice," he told her.

The words caused an unexpected warmth to flow

through her, but she forced herself to respond lightly. "You must have too much time on your hands."

"I wish I did, but even in these preliminary stages, the negotiations are threatening to be intense."

"You should be thrilled—this is what you've been waiting a whole week for."

"I should be," he agreed. "Instead I'm wondering when I might get a chance to see you again."

"We'll get together some time before you head back to Chicago," she said.

He chuckled softly. "I was hoping to see you several times before then."

"I understand that you're busy."

"But I still need to eat," he said. "And so do you. How about meeting for dinner tonight when I finish here?"

"Actually, I already have plans for dinner," she told him.

There was a pause, then he asked, "A date?"

"A birthday party."

"Are you going with a date?"

Her sigh was part amusement and part exasperation. "No. It's a family thing."

"We could get together after," he suggested.

"I don't know how late I'll be."

"All right," he relented. "Enjoy your cake and ice cream while I'm slaving away."

"I'll do that," she said, although she wasn't so sure she would.

Helen stared at the slim gold pen poised over the linen-textured paper. She'd come a long way since she'd first started writing these letters with a dime-store pen on a page torn out of a spiral-bound notebook. Twenty-five years later, the letters weren't any easier to write. If anything, the ritual had become increasingly more difficult and unexpectedly more painful. Whoever said that time heals all wounds had never had to make the choices she had.

My darling daughter,

She didn't notice the sting of tears, a small discomfort compared to the sharper, deeper ache of emptiness in her heart.

Her hand trembled, smudging the ink a little as she set the point to the page again.

I don't know what to say that I haven't already said a dozen times before. I don't know how to explain—

The phone rang; the pen slipped from her grasp.

She glanced at the call display, frowning at the unfamiliar display of numbers. Then it clicked—Tokyo. The merger. Richard.

She slid the paper aside, took a deep breath and picked up the receiver.

"Hello?"

"Helen, it's Richard."

"Hi." Her voice brightened noticeably. Maybe too noticeably. She tried for a more natural tone. "How are things in Tokyo?"

"Things are moving, if a little more slowly than we'd like," he told her.

"Good," she said, her response proof that she was listening to, if not really hearing, him.

There was a pause before he asked, "Is everything okay, Helen?"

"Why wouldn't it be?"

"Because you're at home at eight-thirty on a weekday morning."

"I just needed to get away from the distractions for a while."

"Is Jack still giving you a hard time about the merger?"

She sighed. "No. For once, this has nothing to do with business."

Which was an acknowledgement that there was *something,* and she'd never intended to admit to even that much.

"Is there anything I can do to help?"

She wished there was a way to delegate the grief and guilt to someone else—if only for a little while. But of course she had to suffer the consequences of her own decisions.

"Just take care of the negotiations," she told him.

Chapter Eight

When Mori Taka called for a morning break to take a conference call, Richard took advantage of the reprieve to track Jenny down in the newsroom. He sat in the chair across from her and gestured to the bouquet of balloons on the corner of her desk. "When you told me you were going to a birthday party, you didn't tell me it was yours."

She lifted one shoulder as she clicked to save her document before turning away from the computer screen.

"Happy belated birthday."

"Thanks."

"Why don't you sound very happy?"

"It was my twenty-fifth," she admitted.

He waited a beat, but no further explanation was forthcoming. "Oh, that's right," he said. "I forgot that twenty-five is the *unhappy* birthday."

She managed a smile. "It wasn't the birthday so much as the celebration."

"Not enough pomp and circumstance?"

"On the contrary," she said dryly. "My parents planned this formal occasion with a catered meal and elaborate decorations. There was even a parade of men."

"Is that some kind of Japanese birthday ritual I don't know about?"

She shook her head. "That's my mother's not-so-subtle way of trying to find me a husband. Most of the invited guests were handpicked for their twin virtues of being single and suitable to marry."

He was starting to understand why she sounded less than pleased.

"I want to get married," she admitted. "But I want to fall in love, too. Not that I expect to be swept off my feet, but a little romance would be nice."

He nodded. "You want love and romance, but no sweeping and no kissing."

Her eyes narrowed as she picked up the cup of coffee from her desk and took a long swallow. "You're making fun of me."

"I'm only trying to keep your requirements clear in my mind."

"Don't bother. It has nothing to do with you."

"Of course not," he agreed. "I'm just an interested bystander. But it might be a good idea to make a checklist."

She shook her head, but the hint of a smile tugged at her lips. "You're not helping."

"Maybe you don't really know what you want."

"And you do?"

He shrugged. "My desires are simple."

Now she laughed openly. "Is that an eloquent way of saying you don't want anything more complicated than a warm body in your bed?"

There was a time that her question would have been valid. That had changed before he came to Japan, but somehow getting to know Jenny had changed him even more. "If that was all I wanted, I wouldn't be here."

"Why are you here?"

"I saw the *Tribune* today." He smiled. "Front page headlines and follow-up on page three. Nice work."

"It wasn't the breaking news I originally hoped for, but I was happy with it," she admitted.

"I was thinking I should take you out for dinner to celebrate."

"Tonight?"

"Actually, I was going to suggest tomorrow. Tonight there's a mandatory dinner meeting."

"And I have to attend a showing at a local gallery tomorrow," she told him.

He considered that before asking, "Business or pleasure?"

"Both."

"Do you have a date?"

"No. Nor do I want one," she admitted.

He smiled. "Would it really be so horrible to drag me along?"

"Why would you want to be dragged along?"

"I enjoy spending time with you. Hard to believe, I know. I guess I'm perverse that way."

She lifted an eyebrow. "Any other perversions I should know about?"

"Not at this point in our relationship."

"We don't have a relationship."

"I'm working on it."

"That's the kind of information you should keep to yourself if you want to go to this showing with me."

"One of the things I like most about you is your honesty. You tell it the way it is. I figured I should return the favor."

"It's formal," she warned.

"I'm sure I can find something to wear."

"All right," she finally agreed. "I'll meet you in the hotel lobby at seven."

"That should be good. Mr. Taka promised we would break early tomorrow because of the late meeting tonight."

"How are the negotiations coming?"

"It looks like this might take a while," he admitted. "I'm starting to think we have a fundamental difference of opinion on certain key issues."

"It's a major step for both companies."

He nodded. It would be a big investment for TAKA but Hanson *needed* the merger, and although Jenny probably knew that, it wasn't something he could talk about. His job was to protect the interests of Hanson Media and advertising their desperation—especially to a member of the press— wasn't a good way to do it.

The phone on Jenny's desk buzzed, startling them both.

"Nigel Whitter is on line four," a female voice announced through the speaker.

"Thanks, Kari." Jenny looked at him apologetically. "I have to take this call."

"And I have to get back to the boardroom." He stood up, ready to go. "I'll see you tomorrow night."

"It's not a date," she reminded him.

He grinned. "We'll see."

* * *

He wasn't going to show up.

For all of Richard's claims about wanting to see her and his determined wrangling of an invitation to the event, it had taken nothing more than a message from Chicago to have him change his plans.

Jenny wasn't surprised—his last minute phone call wasn't unexpected. The disappointment was. She mulled over this realization as she wandered through the gallery, an untouched glass of champagne in her hand.

She'd been looking forward to seeing him. As much as she hated to admit it, it was true. She hadn't seen him since his impromptu visit to the newsroom yesterday afternoon, but she'd thought about him—maybe too much.

He'd apologized profusely for the change of plans; she'd assured him it wasn't a problem. He'd promised to meet her at the gallery; she'd told him it wasn't necessary. And yet, she wanted him to come—she wanted to believe that she mattered enough to him that he would make the effort.

She stopped in front of a vibrant seascape in furious shades of purple and red and wondered what it was about her that she was so ready to fall into the same trap all over again. It was the pattern of her life—to want too much and need too deeply.

She tipped her glass to her lips. The champagne was flat and warm, a testament to how long she'd been holding the drink, how long she'd been waiting.

She moved on to study the next display—this one an abstract of gentle blues, soft greens and subtle pinks. It should have been a soothing picture, but the clash of colors was no less violent because of the muted tones. It was a painting you didn't see so much as feel.

She glanced at the discreet placard noting the title of the work. *Summer Passion.*

Now she understood why the picture seemed to speak to her—it reflected so many of the conflicting emotions inside herself. Desires and denials, frustrations and fears, wants and needs. She swallowed another mouthful of warm champagne and turned away.

As she did so, she caught a glimpse of a dark head and broad shoulders. Her heartbeat quickened, then settled again when she realized the man was a stranger.

He's not going to show, she told herself again. It was foolish to set herself up for disappointment by expecting otherwise. It was equally foolish, she knew, to want him to come. She might not be able to deny the desire that sparked whenever he was near, but she had no intention of giving in to it. She refused to open up her heart to yet another man who would only break it.

But beyond the physical attraction she felt, she actually enjoyed spending time with him. After their initial meeting, she'd been determined not to like him. She was certain he was ruthless and arrogant, single-minded and self-absorbed. But over the next few days they'd spent together, she'd found her initial impressions changing.

She didn't doubt he could be ruthless in his business dealings, but he was also thoughtful and kind, as he'd demonstrated in the pleasure he'd found buying gifts for his family. He could be arrogant, but the cockiness was tempered by his self-effacing humor. And he was intelligent, able to converse easily about everything from baseball to world politics.

Okay, he was still pushy, but he was also an interesting and charming man and she was dangerously close to becoming infatuated.

She decided it was a good thing he'd stood her up.

It was after nine o'clock by the time Richard finished his conference call with Helen and made his way to the gallery. After a long day of meetings, he would ordinarily have wanted nothing more than to loosen his tie and put his feet up. Instead, he'd traded his suit for a tux, any hint of weariness overcome by the anticipation of seeing Jenny.

He pushed open the frosted glass door and stepped inside. The gallery was both smaller than he'd expected and more crowded. Silks whispered, jewels glittered and the scent of money hung heavy in the air.

He stood on the fringe of the crowd and scanned the room, searching for her. If he'd thought about it, he might have been concerned by his eagerness. He only thought of Jenny.

And then he found her.

She was wearing a little black dress that clung enticingly to her subtle curves and a pair of skyscraper heels that emphasized shapely calves. Her hair was swept up in some kind of fancy twist, leaving the long, graceful line of her neck bare. Diamonds sparkled at her ears; a matching teardrop pendant drew attention to the shadowy hollow between her breasts.

He accepted a glass of champagne from a passing waiter and stood back for a moment simply enjoying the view— elegant and sophisticated with just a hint of sexy.

His opinion altered dramatically when she turned to speak to the man standing beside her and he realized the dress was more *little* than anything else. It plunged in the back, dipping almost to her waist and revealing a tantalizing expanse of satiny skin. He gulped a mouthful of champagne, but the cool liquid had no effect on the fiery heat suddenly pulsing through him.

He remained in the shadows, watching as she made her way around the room, stopping to chat frequently with people she knew. She shook hands with some, exchanged air kisses with others, embraced a few.

She was in another man's arms now—a bald man with wire-rimmed glasses—and she was smiling at him, her eyes lit with genuine warmth and humor. She tucked her hand into the crook of his arm and led him over to the buffet table. Her companion shook his head when she offered him a plate, but continued to make conversation with her while she piled hors d'oeuvres on her own.

Richard decided he'd hovered in the background long enough.

He knew the exact moment she spotted him, could tell by the way she stilled as their gazes locked across the room. It was as if every muscle in her body grew taut and every nerve stretched tight. He moved toward her, with every step he sensed her nervousness growing along with the sexual tension between them.

She wasn't comfortable with him, he realized. She didn't relax enough to laugh easily or flirt casually. He decided he liked making her uneasy—at least it proved she wasn't indifferent.

He stepped toward them just as he heard Jenny's companion saying, "I'll see you next week, then."

Her only response was a nod, but she waited until the other man had walked away before she turned to him.

"Hello, Jenny."

Her smile was pleasant, if a little cool. "Richard. I didn't think you were coming."

"I told you I would."

"So you did." She took her time in selecting a stuffed mushroom. "You also said you'd be here around eight."

"I got caught up."

"These things happen."

Her response was casual, her tone wasn't.

"You're annoyed with me."

"Of course not," she denied. "I told you not to worry if you couldn't make it."

"I wanted to see you."

Another cool smile. "And now you have."

He plucked a shrimp from her plate, popped it into his mouth.

"Help yourself," she said dryly.

"Thanks." He smiled as he stole another shrimp. "I missed dinner."

"So did I."

He picked up an olive, held it to her lips. She accepted it automatically, her lips brushing his fingertips as she did so. He saw the flare of awareness in her eyes, the flicker of wariness. She definitely wasn't relaxed now. She was tempted, and fighting the temptation.

"I've actually been here a little while," he said.

"How long?"

He smiled. "Long enough to see you flirting with other men."

"What other men?"

"The bald guy with round glasses, the gray-haired man with the diamond on his pinky, the short guy wearing the red bow tie."

"Not that I owe you any explanations, but Ethan is a friend of mine from way back. In fact, I introduced him to his wife. Saburo is a friend of my parents. And Bruce is a copy editor at the paper."

He nodded. "I see."

She tilted her head back to meet his gaze. "What do you see?"

"That you flirt with married men, old men, and co-workers, but you don't flirt with me."

Her only response was a slight furrow between her brows.

"Is it because I make you nervous?"

"You don't make me nervous," she denied.

"Maybe it's not me," he allowed. "Maybe it's the attraction between us."

"Are the negotiations with TAKA stalled again? Because you really do have too much time on your hands if this is the kind of stuff you're dreaming up."

He brushed the back of his hand over her cheek. "I'm not imagining the way your pulse is racing right now."

She pushed his hand away and picked up a cracker.

He decided he wouldn't push the issue—yet.

"I don't know about you," he said. "But this isn't doing anything to ease my hunger. Why don't we go somewhere for dinner?"

She shook her head. "I can't."

He thought she sounded disappointed, or maybe he'd just imagined it.

"There are still several other people I need to see," she

explained. "But there's no reason for you to stay if you don't want to."

He touched her back between her shoulder blades, his palm tingling where it contacted her silky skin. "I want to."

"Why do I think you're not expressing an interest in the art?"

"Because you're a very smart woman." His hand slid lower, to the small of her back, his thumb tracing the skin inside the V-shape cut of the fabric. "I like your dress."

Jenny had chosen it carefully, determined that if he showed up, he'd know exactly what he was missing. But now that he was here, standing close, touching her, his eyes clearly communicating his desire, she wished she'd chosen differently—more conservatively

But she managed a cool smile and a cooler "Thank you."

His fingers trailed upward again, slowly tracing the ridges of her spine. "I can't help but wonder if you wore it for me—or to spite me?"

"I already told you, I didn't expect you'd show up."

"But you knew it would torture me if I did."

Her lips curved just slightly. "Are you feeling tortured?"

"Among other things." He dipped his head toward her and when he spoke again, his voice was low and his breath fanned across her cheek. "Most notably a desire to take you someplace where I can strip that dress from your body and run my hands and lips over every inch of your bare skin."

"In your dreams."

"It's going to happen. Maybe it won't be tonight, maybe it won't be that dress, but it is going to happen."

The heated promise of his words sent a shiver—part fear, part anticipation—through her veins. Thankfully, before she could throw caution to the wind and throw herself into his arms, she spotted her parents across the room.

She turned back to Richard. "Are you picturing me naked right now?" she asked softly.

"I'm trying," he admitted.

"Well, you might want to put some clothes on that mental image before I introduce you to my mom and dad."

Meeting Jenny's parents was the last thing Richard had expected when he'd finessed an invitation to this event. Not that he had any real objection, but he'd been looking forward to some one-on-one with Jenny, not making small talk with strangers.

He'd heard of Harold and Dana Anderson, of course. They were the force behind Anderson International, a group of hotels renowned around the world for their luxurious accommodations and quality of service. They were the destination of choice for movie stars and professional athletes, politicians and royalty—or anyone who expected the best and could afford to indulge.

He recognized the couple from photographs that had appeared in the society pages of newspapers around the world, discussing not just their chain of hotels but their philanthropic works, as well.

Harold Anderson stood about six feet tall, with the build of a professional football player. His dark hair was liberally streaked with gray, his beard more salt than pepper. He was older than Richard would have guessed, probably in his early sixties, but a man to be reckoned with. Not because of his physical size or the wealth his hotel empire had amassed, but because of the sharp intelligence that gleamed in his dark eyes. Eyes that were narrowed on Richard, shrewdly assessing.

Richard wondered if the man knew he had designs on his daughter or if Jenny's father was in the habit of trying to intimidate any man who came too close to his little girl.

He shifted his attention to Dana Anderson. Jenny's mother was of average height, which meant that she was several inches shorter than her daughter, with chin-length blond hair and blue eyes. She wore a glittery silver gown that highlighted her slender figure and a stunning sapphire and diamond choker.

"Jenny." Dana kissed both of her daughter's cheeks. "You look lovely."

"Looks like she bought only half a dress," Harold grumbled. "Probably couldn't afford the rest because she spends her entire paycheck on rent."

"Dad," Jenny said warningly. But there was genuine warmth and affection in her smile as she turned to kiss him, too.

"There's no reason for you not to live at home," her father said. "Or, if you must live downtown, you could at least let us help you out."

"Harold," Dana piped in. "Let's not get into this in front of Jenny's friend."

It was a deliberate prompt for Jenny to make the introductions, which she finally did. "Dad, Mom, meet Richard Warren. Richard, these are my parents, Harold and Dana Anderson."

He shook hands with each of the senior Andersons. "It's nice to meet both of you."

Dana smiled; Harold didn't.

"I didn't realize you were going to be here tonight," Jenny said.

"Neither did I until about an hour ago," her father responded.

Dana patted her husband's arm consolingly. "Art isn't Harold's thing," she told Richard. "But the artist's mother is a friend of mine, so I thought it would be a good opportunity to show our support for Amaya and see Jenny at the same time."

"We wouldn't have to visit with her at public functions if she still lived at home," Harold said again.

Jenny sighed as she tucked her arm into her father's and tipped her head against his shoulder. The gesture of affection seemed to appease him a little.

"We see a lot more of her now than we did when she lived in New York," Dana pointed out.

Jenny smiled at her mother, a wordless expression of gratitude.

"I guess that's true," Harold finally conceded. "And I do sleep better knowing she's not too far, and especially knowing that she's not with—"

"Look," Jenny interrupted. "There's Jonathon and Michiko."

She smiled as she turned to greet the couple who'd just arrived—her brother and a gorgeous Japanese woman with long, silky black hair, dark eyes and a very obviously pregnant belly.

"Mr. Warren." Jonathon said with a nod.

Richard returned the acknowledgment in kind.

"You know each other?" Harold asked.

"We met at the hotel on Saturday," John said.

Richard imagined father and son would be comparing

notes later, trying to figure out his role in Jenny's life and if he was worthy of her. He wasn't bothered because whatever his role, it was only temporary.

"We haven't met," the woman with Jenny's brother said pointedly. "I'm John's wife, Michiko."

"It's a pleasure." He offered an awkward bow, and she smiled at his attempt of a Japanese-style greeting.

"Where's Suki?" Harold asked the newcomers.

Michiko shuddered. "Can't you imagine the damage she could do in a place like this?"

"I was imagining that she might enjoy comparing her technique with the artist's."

"Harold," Dana admonished in a stern whisper, while the others chuckled.

"There are certain similarities," Jenny agreed. "Although I don't think Amaya would appreciate having those pointed out."

"Suki is?" Richard prompted.

"My niece," Jenny told him.

"An incredibly energetic and active four-year-old who doesn't walk when she can run," John elaborated.

Dana smiled. "She reminds me of Jenny at that age," she said fondly.

Harold put his arm around his daughter's shoulders. "You wouldn't guess that this beautiful young woman used to climb trees, collect frogs and make mud pies, would you, Mr. Warren?"

Richard let his gaze skim over the exquisitely dressed woman who'd captivated him from the first moment he'd seen her outside the TAKA boardroom. "I can't say that I would," he agreed.

"I'm sure Richard isn't interested in hearing stories about my childhood," Jenny said.

"Actually, I am interested," he said.

She glared at him. "In any event," she continued as if he hadn't spoken, "I promised to introduce him to some people."

Then she took his arm and began to lead him away.

"It was nice to meet all of you," he said over his shoulder.

"You, too," Dana said.

Michiko smiled.

Harold and John both nodded, apparently reserving judgment.

"I don't recall you promising to make any introductions," he said to Jenny.

"Then I won't bother."

"So why did you really drag me away from your family?"

"Earlier you said something about dinner," she reminded him. "I'm hungry."

"Were you afraid your mother would pull out an album of baby pictures?" he asked. "Although I don't think that purse was big enough for an album, maybe just one or two photos."

"I'm glad you find this amusing."

He grinned as he followed her outside. "I'll bet you were a cute baby."

"I know where there's a great *teppanyaki* just a short walk up the road," she said, pointedly ignoring his comment.

A *teppanyaki*, he knew from his guidebook of Japan, was a steak house. Although his stomach grumbled its agreement with the suggestion, what he really wanted was some time alone with Jenny.

"I have a better idea."

Chapter Nine

"I'm not sure this is a better idea," Jenny said to Richard, pausing outside the main entrance of the hotel.

"Don't you like the food here?"

"I don't like thinking that my father will probably know I'm here with you before we find a table in the restaurant."

"The staff here are very discreet," he told her.

"Of course they are," she agreed. "I'm just not sure the usual policy of nondisclosure applies to the owners' daughter."

"Then it's a good thing we're not going to one of the restaurants." He took her hand to guide her toward the bank of elevators.

"I'm *not* going to your room."

"It's a suite," he said, as if that made a difference. "And I have no evil intentions. I only brought you here so we could share a meal and conversation without interruption."

She eyed him warily. "This from the man who said what he liked most about my dress was the idea of taking it off me."

He grinned. "It's still true. It's also true that I won't make love with you until you want it as much as I do."

"It isn't going to happen."

"Not tonight," he agreed easily.

Not ever. She wanted to speak those words; she wanted to mean them. But she was no longer certain about anything where Richard Warren was concerned.

The elevator dinged to announce its arrival.

"Are you coming?" he asked.

"Only because I'm hungry," she told him.

He smiled. "I didn't expect anything else."

But Jenny was still wary when she stepped into the car. Not because she didn't trust Richard. He'd been honest about what he wanted from the very beginning, and she believed that he didn't have any ulterior motives for inviting her to his room. She was more worried about her weakening resolve where he was concerned.

"Tell me more about your family," Richard suggested after their meals had been delivered.

"You've met them all except Suki," Jenny said. "What do you want to know?"

"Is your father as protective of you as your brother?"

"He can be even more so," she admitted. "But he and Mom traveled a lot, so John took on a lot of parental responsibility where I was concerned. I think he actually enjoyed intimidating the guys I dated in high school."

"Did he ever beat anyone up for you?"

"Worried?" she teased.

"Maybe."

Jenny laughed softly. "No. In fact, I don't think he's ever thrown a punch. Even when we were kids, John always made smart choices. He never gave our parents a moment's worry, while I tested them constantly. Breaking curfew, sneaking out of the house, smoking, drinking—"

"Why?"

Her smile faded; her eyes clouded. "To prove what I thought I already knew—that I was unlovable. To see if they would give me away, too."

"Give you away?" he echoed, genuinely baffled by her statement. "Why would you ever think they'd do that?"

"Because my mother did." She set her chopsticks down and pushed her plate away.

Suddenly the pieces clicked into place. "You were adopted?"

She nodded. "I always knew it, but I didn't really understand what it meant until I was in sixth grade and a new girl joined our class. Wendy was in foster care because her mother wasn't capable of raising her. She'd been in and out of several different homes over the years. At one time, she'd had foster parents who'd wanted to adopt her. But her mother refused to sign the papers, claiming she loved her too much to ever let her go."

The hurt and confusion were evident in her tone. "And you assumed, because your mother had put you up for adoption, it meant she didn't love you."

"It seems the obvious explanation," she said.

He shook his head, unable to believe that this incredible woman could harbor such deep-rooted doubts about herself. "I don't think it's obvious at all. Maybe she loved you too much to ruin your life by letting you be shuffled in and out of other people's homes."

"Maybe." But she clearly didn't believe it. "In any case, I figured if my own mother could turn her back on me, my adoptive parents would, too. So I started acting out, pushing them to the point where I was sure they would throw their hands into the air and me into the streets."

"But they didn't."

"No. They threw me into counseling instead." She shook her head. "Even then, they didn't abandon me. They sat by my side through each of the sessions, wanting only to help. I yelled at them and swore at them, and they never wavered."

"They love you."

She smiled. "I finally got that. And with the realization came the guilt and a determination to make amends, to make them proud of me so they'd never regret everything they'd given me."

"Was your brother adopted, too?"

"Yeah. He was four years old when his biological parents were killed in a car accident. Two years later, the Andersons decided he should have a sibling."

"And that's when they adopted you?"

She nodded. "I don't know whether it's that he got there first, or maybe it's because he actually looks a little bit like our mom, but he just always seemed to fit into the family while I never quite felt like I did."

"I'm not sure I ever fit into my family, either," he told her.

"But at least you know them. I have no clue about mine."

"Yes, you do," he insisted. "Even though you're not related by blood, you're still a family. That was obvious in the few minutes I saw you together."

She was silent, considering.

"But if you really want to know your biological family,"

he continued, "it seems that would be easy enough to arrange through the agency that adopted you out or—"

She shook her head, cutting him off. "I used to think about it," she admitted. "But then I'd feel guilty for even considering it. I know I'm lucky to have two parents who love me—why would I risk screwing that up by searching for a mother who already rejected me?"

"It seems to me that your doubts and insecurities are screwing up your relationship with your family anyway."

She sighed. "I just wish I was more like Jonathon, more like our parents—quiet and serious. As a child, I had a tendency to do everything at full volume."

He smiled. "You still do."

She frowned.

"You carry yourself with poise and elegance, but there's an energy around you—a constancy of motion even when you're standing still."

"And I thought I'd outgrown that."

He brushed his fingers over the back of her hand. "I don't think passion is a character flaw."

"Passion?" Jenny asked the question skeptically as she pulled her hand away. But even then, she could still feel the warmth of his touch on her skin, and she yearned to feel his touch on every part of her body.

"It's there," he told her. "Tightly controlled and all the more intriguing because of that control. It makes a man wonder what might happen if he ever managed to unleash it."

She pushed her chair away from the table. "I have to go. I have an early meeting with my editor tomorrow."

He stood up with her. "What are you doing Friday night?"

"I'm busy."

"Are you? Or are you trying to put some distance between us?"

"I'm going out with Samara," she said, which they both knew only answered the first part of his question. But she breathed a sigh of relief that she had legitimate plans, because she knew that she was in danger of getting in too deep with Richard and she desperately needed some of that distance he'd mentioned. Better yet, she needed him to finish up the negotiations and go back to Chicago—that would establish a lot of distance.

"Okay," he said. "But that doesn't mean I'm giving up."

"I'm not trying to challenge you."

"I know." He smiled and brushed his thumb over her bottom lip. She felt it tremble, ever so slightly, and could only hope that he didn't notice the instinctive response.

"Come on," he said. "I'll walk you home."

Jenny shook her head. She needed that distance now, before she did something crazy. "I'll take a taxi."

"Are you sure?"

"It'll be quicker," she said. "It's already late and I really want to get to bed. Home to bed. To sleep."

He smiled at the hasty amendments. "Okay."

She exhaled, silently relieved by his agreement. "Good night, Richard."

He caught her hand as she reached for the handle of the door. "Do you really think I'm going to let you go without kissing you tonight?"

"We agreed—"

"The rules are changing," he said.

She didn't have a chance to brace herself before his lips brushed against hers. But even as she yielded to the kiss, she knew nothing could have prepared her for the feel of his mouth on hers, the confident mastery of his lips, the heat of her own desire.

Her lips parted and his tongue skimmed over hers with slow teasing strokes. She couldn't think or reason, only respond. And the immediacy and intensity of her response stunned her. It was more than want—it was an aching need, a desperate yearning.

His hands moved up her back, sliding over the bare expanse of skin from her waist to her neck and back again. She felt her skin heat, her blood pulse, her bones melt.

He pressed her against the door, his body hard against hers, and incredibly arousing. She shivered, suddenly afraid of the growing need she felt inside, and of wanting more than he could give her.

When he finally eased away, she drew in a long, shaky breath and waited for the world to steady beneath her feet.

"What was that?" she asked, sounding breathless and dazed.

The way he looked at her was just as arousing as a touch, unrestrained desire blazing from the depths of his blue eyes. "That," he said, rubbing his thumb over her bottom lip, "was the proper way to end a date."

She swallowed. "I told you it wasn't a date."

His smile was slow and sexy and just a little bit smug. "You were wrong."

Jenny was glad she had plans with Samara and some other friends for Friday night. She'd been spending far too much time with Richard Warren lately, and when she wasn't with him, she was thinking about him. Even more than usual after their evening at the art gallery and the late dinner they'd shared in his suite. Or maybe it was the kiss that was to blame.

It would be easy to explain away her fascination as lust. There was no denying that at least part of the attraction she felt was physical. And maybe, if she'd taken Samara's advice and slept with him a week ago, it might have ended there. It wasn't that simple anymore.

Her feelings for Richard already went deeper than desire. She enjoyed being with him and talking to him, and she found herself missing him when he wasn't around. When he'd asked her about her plans for tonight, she'd been tempted to invite him to join her friends—to show him a karaoke bar as yet another aspect of Japanese culture. She knew no one would have objected to his presence. But she also knew she was just looking for an excuse to see him again. And after the kiss they'd shared in his hotel room—

Well, she'd already spent far too much time thinking about that kiss. What she needed was a night out with friends to forget about Richard Warren.

And it was working, too. Her thoughts strayed to him only once every few minutes instead of a few times every minute. She concentrated instead on the group of people around her. There were about a dozen of them—friends and coworkers and significant others—in the private room they rented once a month to indulge in silly fun without making fools of themselves in front of strangers.

Malcolm had the microphone now and was squinting at the lyrics on the screen and struggling more than a little with the tune of an old Beatles song. Jenny tapped her foot to the beat of the music.

Yes, this was exactly what she needed—time and distance from Richard. Because staying away from the sexy lawyer was the only way to guarantee she would stay out of his bed.

* * *

Richard made his way up the stairs and down the hall to find the correct room number. When he'd called Samara to ask about her plans with Jenny, she'd promised they would be here tonight. He hadn't realized it was a karaoke bar, and he hadn't expected to find Jenny on stage.

He stood at the back of the room for a moment, captivated by her. He recognized the song, vaguely. A pop tune from several years back about believing in life after love. She was belting out the lyrics with obvious enthusiasm, singing as she did everything else—with intensity and passion.

He felt the stir of desire. In the past couple of weeks, he'd grown accustomed to the basic physical reaction of his body to her presence. It was the less familiar and distinctly uncomfortable yearning for something more that bothered him.

It had been a mistake to kiss her again. He'd had a taste, a glimpse—it wasn't nearly enough. He wanted more. He wanted everything.

It was only his promise to her, his reassurance that he would wait until she was ready, that had made him pull away while he was still thinking clearly enough to do so.

She affected him on a level he didn't think he'd ever experienced before and wasn't sure he was ready for. If he was smart, he would turn around now and walk back out the door before she ever knew he was here.

It was further proof of the power she held over him that he didn't turn around. Instead, he made his way across the room, toward a vacant chair in front of the stage where Samara and some others were watching.

He slipped into the empty chair beside Jenny's roommate. Samara smiled at him. "You made it."

"And I only got lost once."

She laughed and poured him a glass of beer from the pitcher on the table. "That's impressive."

Richard accepted the drink, his eyes on the stage as Jenny finished her song to a smattering of applause.

She bowed, then set the microphone back in the stand and gestured for Samara to take the stage. As her friend did so, Jenny took her now vacated seat.

"You were fabulous," Richard told her.

"Thank you." She accepted the compliment as warily as his presence. "What are you doing here?"

"Samara invited me."

Jenny sipped again. "When?"

"When I called her last night to find out what you were doing tonight." He picked up the pitcher to pour Jenny a drink.

"Thanks." She leaned forward and dropped her voice so only he would hear. "But I'm not going to get drunk and let you seduce me."

"I don't want you drunk," he told her. "I want you coherent and willing."

She sat back again. "You'd have better luck if you tried for drunk."

He smiled and let his gaze drop to her mouth, remembering how soft it had been under his, how incredibly responsive. "I don't think so." He twined an errant strand of hair around his finger and tugged gently. "I do want you, Jenny."

He saw the quick flash of heat in her eyes, but she responded coolly. "Yes, we've already established that."

"I think you want me, too."

"I'm not going to deny there's a basic physical attraction. But I wasn't lying when I said I don't do casual relationships."

"My feelings for you are anything but casual," he told her. "They're powerful and intense and lately they've been driving me to distraction."

The words caused a quick thrill of pleasure to course through her, an instinctive reaction which fueled her annoyance. He was a lawyer—it was his job to find the right words to get what he wanted. She refused to let his words sway her.

"You're just not used to having any woman turn you down."

He shifted his chair closer, his thigh brushing against hers beneath the table. "Could we forget about everyone else and just focus on us for a minute?"

"I'd rather focus on the music," she said. "This is one of my favorite songs."

"Okay." His leg rubbed against hers again. "But we'll get back to this."

It was a promise that made her heartbeat quicken.

Samara finished her song and came back to the table. "Gabe's up next."

"I hope it's a short one this time," Jenny said, then grimaced as the first notes of Don McLean's "American Pie" filled the room.

"We're going to need another pitcher of beer, Kazuo." Samara spoke to the man beside her. Then to Richard she said, "Do you sing?"

He shook his head. "Not in public."

"Everyone has to sing," Jenny said. "It's a commitment you make when you walk through the door."

"It's not exactly a rule," Samara said. "It's more an expectation."

"Of course, if you're uncomfortable with the thought of getting up on stage, you can sneak out now," Jenny told him.

Richard winced as the singer hit a note he'd never heard before. He had some concerns about making a fool of himself, but he was confident he could at least perform better than what they were hearing at present. "I don't think my Japanese experience would be complete without at least a little karaoke."

"I told her you wouldn't buck at a challenge," Samara said.

"Balk," Jenny told her, scanning the list of song choices. "A buck is a male deer or slang for a dollar."

Samara sighed. "Five years of college in America, and I still have trouble with the language."

"Your English is a lot better than my Japanese will ever be," Richard told her.

She smiled her gratitude as the man who'd gone to get more beer returned with two pitchers. He set them on the table, then sat down beside Samara and laid his arm across her shoulders. It might have been a casual display of affection, but Richard recognized the warning in his eyes and knew it was a blatant display of territoriality.

Samara rolled her eyes, obviously interpreting the gesture the same way. "This is Richard Warren," she said. "He's the lawyer from Chicago that I was telling you about. Richard, this is Kazuo."

"You're Jenny's friend?" Kazuo asked.

He wasn't so sure Jenny would consider him a *friend* or that he wanted to be classified as such, but he guessed it was a suitable title at present. He nodded and offered his hand.

Kazuo shook it, his grip more firm than friendly.

"Richard's a karaoke virgin," Jenny leaned over to inform the other man.

He smirked.

"I don't think anyone should have to go it alone their first time," Samara said, coming to his defense.

Kazuo stroked his fingers down her arm. "Maybe Jenny could help ease him into it."

Jenny was shaking her head before Kazuo finished speaking. "I'm sure Richard can handle it on his own."

He set down his empty glass and leaned closer to her. "I can," he agreed. "But I think I would enjoy being initiated by someone with so much more experience."

She glared at him. "You're falling right into her trap."

"I don't mind being trapped with you."

It wasn't the words so much as the tenor of his voice that made her realize there was a lot more going on beneath the surface of their conversation.

"I've got it," Samara announced triumphantly, already punching buttons into the machine to program her selection.

Gabe had finally finished his song and handed the microphone to Kazuo, who passed it to Richard. "You're on."

Richard stood up and took Jenny's hand.

"I'm going to kill Samara," she muttered.

"I like her," he said.

"Then why don't you sing with her?"

"Because I also like all my body parts in the right places, and her boyfriend seemed a little too eager to rearrange them."

She smiled at that. "Kazuo's like a big dog—all bark and no bite."

"Good to know."

"The rest of this crowd is a different story," she warned. "Do you think you can handle it?"

"I'm sure I can stumble along if you lead the way."

Jenny recognized the opening notes of the song and decided that she might forgive Samara for this—someday. At least it wasn't a sentimental ballad about endless love or something equally nauseating. She glanced over at Richard. "You could probably still make a break for the door."

"Not a chance."

There was something in his smile, a distinctly sensual heat underlying the casual curve of his lips. It threw her off balance and made her miss her cue. Then she had to rush the first line to catch up.

Richard's smile widened, as if he sensed her discomfiture and knew he was the cause of it. His gaze lingered on hers for a moment before it shifted to the monitor.

His singing unnerved her as much as the smile. She should have guessed he wouldn't have risked getting up on stage unless he could carry a tune, but she hadn't been prepared for how good he was. He had an incredible voice—strong and sure, even singing the sappy lyrics of an old Sonny and Cher tune.

This time when he smiled, she smiled back.

He was being a really good sport despite having been coerced to participate and it was, after all, harmless fun.

And then he touched her.

In the middle of the stage, under the lights, he'd reached out and stroked his hand down her arm to link with hers as he sang. It was as if the words were intended only for her, and everyone else seemed to fade away.

Suddenly it wasn't just fun anymore. It was fun and dangerous, and the emotions swirling inside her were intense and chaotic—fear and need, wariness and wanting.

She saw the reflection of her own desire in his eyes, but his eyes were unclouded by other emotions. It was simple for him—he wanted her and he intended to have her. He'd already stated that intention clearly and unequivocally.

It wasn't that easy for Jenny. She knew if she allowed

herself to engage in a physical relationship with him, her heart would inevitably become involved. She wasn't capable of separating her body from her emotions.

She sang her lines automatically, as her mind scrambled.

How had this happened to her? How was it possible to feel so much so soon? How had she let herself become involved when she knew he would only be in Tokyo a few weeks? What happened to the distance she'd vowed to establish? The only distance between them now was a few inches, and that space was filled with simmering heat that was already melting the last of her resolve.

It wasn't until the sound of clapping penetrated the heavy throb of blood in her ears that she realized the song was over.

She tore her gaze from his and forced a smile as she bowed to her friends. She heard someone—Samara, she would bet—calling for an encore. But Jenny was already off the stage, dropping her microphone on the table.

She made her way down the stairs, pushed through the door and onto the sidewalk. She started to walk with no destination in mind, propelled by a desperate need to breathe, to think.

But all she could think was that she wanted him. There was no point in trying to deny it any longer. From the moment he'd walked into the bar, she'd known it was too late to hold back any longer.

She wasn't ready for this. She wasn't eager to jump into another dead-end relationship.

Richard was only going to be in Tokyo a few more weeks—a month at the most. But right now she couldn't think of a single reason not to take advantage of every minute they might have together over the next month.

No reason except that her heart had been broken too

many times already. She simply didn't have the experience or sophistication to indulge in a casual affair and her heart was too fragile for anything more.

"Jenny."

She wasn't surprised to hear him call her name. She'd left the bar in a last ditch effort for sanity, knowing that if he followed, there would be no turning away. Not this time.

She stopped, turned to face him. "I just needed some air."

Richard took her hands; her heart stuttered.

In that moment, she knew everything was about to change. She was done fighting with herself. She'd made a list as long as her arm of all the reasons he was completely wrong for her. Okay, it was really one reason that she'd written over and over again—because he would be going back to Chicago soon.

She refused to get involved with someone who would soon be more than six thousand miles away.

But while the rational part of her brain understood that a relationship with Richard was doomed to failure, that part was no match for her need. For days they'd been building toward this moment. The moment when she forgot all the reasons they were completely wrong for each other and let herself get lost in the passion she knew they would discover together.

"What's wrong?"

She shook her head again, one last ditch effort to regain her sanity. "Nothing. Really. It's crazy. *I'm* crazy." She laughed. "It must have been the lights."

"What must have been the lights?" He asked the question patiently, as if he already knew the answer.

Of course, he did. He'd been taking it slow to give her a chance to accept what he'd said almost from the beginning was inevitable.

"Short-circuiting my brain," she answered.

He brushed his thumbs over her knuckles—a casual yet somehow sensual gesture that made her ache to feel his touch all over her body.

She swallowed before admitting, "I was actually thinking of asking you to come home with me."

He drew her closer, one corner of his mouth tilting up in a half smile. "Thinking about it?"

She tipped her head back to look at him and said again. "It was a crazy thought."

After a long moment, he finally nodded. "You're right. And if you'd asked, I would have had to say *no*."

Emotions swirled again. Surprise and regret. Relief and disappointment. Hurt that she could have misread him and the situation. Except that when she lifted her gaze to his again, the stark desire in his eyes conflicted with his response.

She could feel the heat emanating from his body, feel the sizzle of passion that matched her own.

"Because it's crazy?" she asked.

He smiled. "Because my hotel is closer."

Chapter Ten

Jenny pushed Richard's jacket over his shoulders, letting it drop to the floor. She yanked at his tie and tossed it aside. Passion was building, burning, inside her. She started on the buttons of his shirt, fumbling as he dipped his head and pressed his lips to the tender skin at the base of her throat.

She shivered in response to the deliciously erotic tingles that rocketed through her body. His fingers had made quick work of her buttons and his lips continued to trail kisses along the ridge of her collarbone, then over the slope of her breast. Her head fell back against the door as his teeth closed over her nipple through the lace of her bra.

It wasn't enough for either of them. He unfastened the front clasp and pushed the cups aside to cradle her breasts in his palms. His thumbs traced lazy circles around the peaks, moving with tantalizing slowness. She was trembling now, her body pulsating with desire. Then his mouth fastened on her breast, his tongue rasping against the nipple, and the pulse grew stronger, more insistent.

He slid her skirt and her panties over her hips, down the length of her incredibly long legs, adding them to the growing pile of discarded clothing that littered the floor. Then he stepped back to look at her. Except for a pair of stay-up stockings and heels, she was naked, while he still had most of his clothes on. But the blatant appreciation in his eyes obliterated any lingering sense of shyness.

"Richard." It was a demand as much as a plea.

Finally, his lips covered hers in a kiss that was hot and hungry and all encompassing. There was no tentative exploration, no soft seduction. There was just heat and hunger, an escalating passion that could no longer be denied as his tongue slid between her parted lips to tangle with her own.

She reached for him, finished unfastening the buttons on his shirt and parted the material to reveal the firm expanse of his chest. Her palms slid over the smooth hard skin, reveling in the muscular contours she would never have guessed were hidden beneath the business suits he habitually wore.

Her hands moved over him greedily, almost desperately. Had she ever wanted anyone so much? Had she ever been wanted the way he seemed to want her?

She banished these thoughts from her mind. She didn't want to think or question, she only wanted to feel. She slid her hand down into the front of his pants, heard his sharp inhalation as she wrapped her fingers around the hard length of him.

He dragged his lips from hers. "I promised myself that if I actually got you up here, I would take my time with you," he said.

"I just want you to take me." She started to push his pants over his hips.

He put his hands over hers, halting her movements. "Condom," he said. "I've got one in my pocket."

She lifted an eyebrow. "I'm not sure if I'm grateful you're prepared or offended you took it for granted I'd be here."

He dipped his head again, nibbled on the lobe of her ear. "Let's just say I was cautiously optimistic after we said goodbye Wednesday night."

"Then I'll say thank you." She brushed her lips against his as she took the packet from his hand. Her mouth still thoroughly occupied with his, she managed to tear open the wrapper and roll the prophylactic into place. She swallowed his moan as her fingers slid down the length of him.

He broke the kiss to press his lips to the side of her throat. "It seems, Jenny Anderson, that you aren't quite what I expected."

She smiled. "Disappointed?"

His only response was to capture her mouth again as he thrust into her.

She gasped, a combination of shock and pleasure, as he filled her. He lifted her legs to wrap them around his waist. She locked her ankles together, anchoring herself to him. The polished wood of the door was smooth and cool against her back, and she braced herself against it as she tilted her hips to pull him deeper inside.

Richard groaned into her mouth, his fingers digging into her hips to still her impatient rocking. "I'm trying to maintain some degree of control here."

She nipped at his shoulder, then soothed the gentle bite with her tongue. "Control is overrated."

He slowly withdrew from her, then sank in again. She gasped.

"Prove it," he challenged.

He moved out and in, deliberately rubbing against the sensitive nub at her center.

She felt her body tense as her mind struggled to follow the thread of conversation. Her breath was coming in shallow gasps now, her fingernails biting into his back.

"Let yourself go, Jenny."

She couldn't seem to do anything else as the first climax swamped her, the waves of her release crashing one into another, each stronger and longer than the previous, until her skin was damp and her entire body was shuddering.

Richard had never seen anything more beautiful than Jenny lost in the throes of passion. It was almost enough to send him spiraling over the edge with her. But not yet.

He braced his hands on the door and fought to hold on to the last vestiges of his control. The clenching of her muscles around him was almost more than he could stand, but he was determined to show her more. When her trembling had subsided, he wrapped his arms around her and carried her to the bed.

He lowered her onto the mattress and knelt over her, still buried inside her.

"Why—"

He brushed his lips over hers, gently this time. "Because I want to make love with you properly."

She smiled. "I didn't think there was anything improper about what we were doing."

"Maybe not," he agreed. "But I couldn't hold you up and do this..."

He dipped his head and took the peak of her breast in his mouth to suckle deeply.

She moaned.

"Or this…"

He slid a hand between their bodies to the soft tangle of curls at the apex of her thighs.

She gasped.

"Again," he said.

She shook her head. "I can't—I don't—"

"Again," he repeated, driving her ruthlessly up and over the peak again, proving that she could.

He crushed his mouth down on hers, swallowing her cries of pleasure. His own needs refused to be denied any longer, and as he drove into her slick, pulsing heat, he plunged over the final, ultimate peak with her.

"I'm sorry." Jenny's words broke the silence.

Richard propped himself up on an elbow to look down at the woman lying naked beside him. She looked sleepily satisfied, the remnants of a smile tilting the corners of her mouth. She certainly didn't look sorry.

"For what?" he asked.

"Holding out for so long."

He brushed his lips over hers. "I'd say it was worth the wait."

Her lips curved. "Definitely."

"Although that's not to say I want to wait another ten days before we do it again."

She snuggled closer, sliding one long slender leg between his, the tips of her breasts grazing his chest. "What kind of time frame did you have in mind?"

"About another ten minutes," he promised.

Her smile widened and she wriggled against him. His body immediately responded to the seductive movement. He'd barely finished having her, and he already wanted her again.

"Ten minutes?" she challenged.

"Maybe less." He flipped her onto her back and rolled on top of her, capturing her lips, kissing his way down her throat. "I wanted you from the first minute I saw you," he told her. "Just like this—naked in my bed."

She gasped when his lips fastened over her breast, sighed when his tongue swirled around her nipple. "Do you always get…what you want?"

"Usually." He moved to her other breast to minister the same treatment. "Because when it's something that really matters, I don't give up."

Then he kissed her. "You matter, Jenny."

"Don't say things like that," she pleaded softly.

"Why?" He kissed her again, longer, lingering. "Were you hoping this was just sex?"

"Maybe." She shifted, drawing her knees up to bracket his hips, opening for him. "It would make things simpler."

He unwrapped another condom, then groaned when he slid into her and found she was hot and wet, as ready as he was all over again.

"This isn't going to be simple," he promised. "Not for either of us."

Richard awoke to the sound of the curtains being pulled open and the glare of sunlight streaming through the windows. He threw his arm over his eyes. "How can it be morning when I haven't had any sleep?"

"Because the earth continues to revolve whether you're

ready for it or not." Jenny sounded surprisingly awake and cheerful although she couldn't have had any more sleep than he did.

They'd barely let go of one another through the night. If they weren't making love, they were getting ready to make love or cuddling together after just having finished making love. He'd thought it would be enough to have her once. That after he'd had her in his bed he'd be able to get her out of his mind. Instead, he wanted her more.

"And if you opened your eyes," she continued, "you'd see that it's a beautiful day."

"I'd be more willing to believe that if you were still in bed with me," he told her.

"If I was still in bed with you, we might miss out on the entire day."

"Why is that a bad thing?"

She chuckled softly as she tugged the covers away from him. "Come on. I've ordered up breakfast, but you probably have time for a quick shower before it gets here."

He snagged her wrist, tumbled her back down onto the bed beside him. "What's the hurry?"

"It's almost nine o'clock."

"But it's Saturday, right?" He wasn't entirely clear—he'd lost himself in her so completely time had faded away. It could have been hours or days or weeks.

"Yes, it's Saturday." Amusement was evident in her tone. "And there's somewhere very special I want to take you today."

"You could take me to paradise without either of us having to leave this room."

"Let's start with Lake Sai."

"Where's that?"

"It's one of the five lakes of Mount Fuji and it has the most spectacular view."

He smiled. "I'm liking the view from here right now."

"Have you ever seen the sun rise behind Mount Fuji?" she challenged.

"I can't say that I have," he admitted.

"Well, tomorrow morning you're going to. And I promise it will be unlike anything you've ever seen."

Somehow she managed to make the prospect of getting up at daybreak appealing. Or maybe it was just the idea of being with her. And if that was how she wanted to spend her weekend, he would oblige her.

Then it hit him—Saturday.

He swore softly.

Jenny frowned. "What's the matter?"

"It's Saturday."

"Yes, I believe we've already established that."

"Helen's coming into town today," he said. "And I'm supposed to go with her to some cocktail party thing tonight."

"Oh." She smiled, but he could tell it was forced. "Well, we'll go some other time then."

"I'm sorry, Jenny."

"It's okay. I shouldn't have assumed that you were free."

But he could see the disappointment in her eyes and felt like a heel for putting it there.

"If I had a choice—" he broke off.

Why didn't he have a choice? Why did he need to be at this reception? It was a purely social event—there would be no business decisions made, no legal expertise required. And it certainly wasn't as if Helen needed him to hold her hand. She might not be pleased by his last-minute change of plans, but he'd rather face her displeasure than the resignation in Jenny's eyes.

From what she'd told him about her childhood and her previous relationships, he knew that her biggest insecurity was feeling as though she was always second best. No one had ever put her first and now, after one night together, Richard was doing the same thing—subordinating her wants to the demands of his career. And the worst part of it was that Jenny wasn't even surprised or angry, as she had every right to be. She'd simply accepted his decision, as if she'd expected he would disappoint her.

The knock at the door signaled the arrival of their breakfast. Richard signed for the meal, then sat at the small table across from Jenny.

She toyed with her food, sipped her coffee.

"How do you get to Lake Sai?"

She frowned at the question as she refilled her cup with coffee. "Car or train."

"Do you have a car or should we rent one?"

"I have a car."

He nodded. "Okay, then I'll take my shower so we can get going."

"Going where?"

"To Mount Fuji to see the sunrise."

"I thought you had plans—"

"I can change them."

He watched the emotions that crossed her face—surprise, pleasure, a flicker of guilt, before she pushed away from the table.

"But your boss—"

"Helen will understand." He stood up and crossed the room to where she was standing.

"I appreciate the offer," she said, "but you don't have to—"

"I want to," he interrupted.

He put his arms around her "—I want to spend the day with you—" pressed his lips to hers "—and the night—" kissed her again "—and all of tomorrow."

Jenny negotiated the tight curves of the winding road with an ease that indicated familiarity—and a speed that made Richard nervous. "This road seems awfully narrow for two-way traffic."

"Don't worry," she told him. "It's a private lane and no one else will be here this weekend."

"Didn't you tell me that we were going to a hotel?"

She shook her head. "I said we were staying overnight."

It was a clarification that told him little. "Staying where?"

They rounded another curve where the trees suddenly gave way to a clearing, highlighting the long low building made of rough-hewn logs.

Jenny pulled up beside the building and parked her car. "My parents' cabin."

He eyed the structure warily. "Did you happen to mention to your parents that you were coming up here?"

"Not specifically." She opened her door and stepped out of the car, linking her hands together over her head, stretching her arms toward the sky.

Richard reluctantly got out of the car, accepting it was necessary to continue their conversation even though he wasn't convinced that the smartest course of action might not be to turn around and return to Tokyo. "What if your parents decide to come up here this weekend?"

"They won't." She popped the trunk; he grabbed their bags. "My brother or I use it a lot more than they do. And with Mich being so close to the end of her pregnancy, she and John haven't been venturing too far out of the city."

He could only hope she was right. He knew neither her father nor her brother would take kindly to finding her snuggled up in the cabin with Richard. On the other hand, spending the weekend snuggled up with Jenny might make any consequences worthwhile.

"Come on," Jenny said, leading him around to the front of the cabin.

They dropped their bags inside, then went through the cabin opening up the windows. There were three bedrooms, one obviously a master with a king-size bed and ensuite, another with a double bed and dresser, and the last contained a set of narrow bunks, a toy chest and a bookshelf. There was also a second bathroom, a moderate-sized kitchen/eating area, and a spacious family room with a stone floor-to-ceiling fireplace. It was rustic and simply furnished, yet also warm and inviting.

"It's not fancy but it's private," Jenny told him.

"I like it," he said.

"You haven't even seen the best part yet."

Richard followed her back outside, down a well-worn path through the trees toward the lake. Although the mountain was visible from his hotel window on a clear day, that distant glimpse hadn't prepared him for the spectacular majesty of Mount Fuji up close. As they stepped into the clearing at the water's edge, his only thought was—she was right about the view.

"It's…incredible."

She smiled, obviously pleased by his reaction. "I've never been anywhere that fills me with the same sense of peace and tranquility as this spot right here."

Considering how much of the globe she'd seen, that was quite an endorsement. His travel experience was much more limited, but he agreed with her assessment wholeheartedly.

The smooth and glossy surface of the lake gave the impression of a mirror provided by nature solely for the purpose of reflecting the towering mountain above. The trees stood tall and proud all around, silent guardians of this natural paradise where the only sounds were the crickets chirping and the birds singing, and the only scents were of damp earth and fresh pine.

Richard didn't consider himself a religious person, but there was something almost spiritual about this place, a sense of magic surrounded it.

"I can see why you love it," he said. "I imagine your friends are always angling for invitations to come here with you."

"Except for Samara, I've never brought anyone with me," she admitted.

He didn't ask why, and she didn't volunteer that information. Perhaps they were both wary of the answer, unprepared to deal with the implications. Instead, he said softly, "Thank you for sharing this with me."

"You're welcome."

She smiled at him again, a smile of warmth and companionship and affection. And in that moment, she was simply too tempting to resist.

Jenny's breath caught in her throat as his lips brushed over hers. Unlike the insatiable passion they'd shared through the night, this was different. Softer, gentler, deeper. Or maybe it wasn't so much the kiss as the emotions churning inside her.

She hadn't known it was possible to feel both secure and vulnerable, except that in the warm strength of his arms she couldn't separate one feeling from the other. It was exhilarating and intimidating, tempting and terrifying all at the same time. It was also frustrating that no matter how hard she tried, she couldn't seem to keep her emotions in check.

She knew he cared about her, and that he would take care with her. But she also knew that she had no protection against him, no shield for her heart. She was in danger here—teetering on the edge of love, desperately trying to regain her balance. But every minute with Richard pushed her a little further toward the precipice.

She'd thought she had a choice, that she'd made a conscious decision to be with him. But after having spent the night in his arms, she knew the truth. There had never been a choice, only a destiny.

Being with him, loving him, were inevitable—as necessary as breathing.

Losing him was, she knew, just as certain.

Chapter Eleven

Richard didn't know what time it was when Jenny nudged his shoulder, he only knew that when he cracked open an eyelid it was still dark and, therefore, obviously not morning. He tugged the sheet up and snuggled deeper into the mattress.

"If you don't get up, you're going to miss the sunrise," she warned.

"It'll happen again tomorrow."

"But we won't be here tomorrow," she reminded him.

When he failed to respond, she nudged him again.

"I'm getting the impression that you're not a morning person," she said, but she sounded more amused than dissuaded.

"I'm not." He pulled the pillow over his head. "Wake me up at noon."

"Okay. But you'll miss seeing me dance naked on the lakeshore."

He shoved the pillow aside. "Naked?"

She laughed. "Come on, I've got coffee on."

"Naked sounded a lot more appealing than coffee," he grumbled, but he sat up and swung his legs over to the floor.

"Let's start with coffee," she said.

While Jenny was gone, he pulled on a pair of shorts over his briefs, then tugged a T-shirt over his head. He sniffed the air, inhaling deeply the fresh aroma of java.

"Thanks." He accepted the mug she offered and gulped several mouthfuls of coffee before he could focus his sleepy gaze on her. She'd already showered and was dressed in a long, flowing skirt and a sleeveless V-neck blouse. She looked wide awake, refreshed and stunningly beautiful.

He didn't care what time it was, he'd wake up happy every morning if he woke up with Jenny beside him.

The thought jolted him awake more effectively than a whole pot of coffee. Whatever fantasies had snuck into his subconscious while he'd slept beside her in the night needed to be exorcised. He wasn't in a position to commit to anything more than a temporary affair—a mutually pleasurable diversion—and they both knew what was between them couldn't last. His business in Tokyo would be concluded in a few weeks, then he'd be on his way back to Chicago. Except that the prospect of going home wasn't quite so appealing to him now.

He gulped another mouthful of coffee and renewed his resolve not to think beyond the present. "Let's go see this sunrise."

But when he followed her out of the cabin, only the

slightest hint of light defined the edge of the horizon, leaving everything else in complete darkness.

"This is sunrise?" he muttered.

Jenny took his hand and led him down toward the water. "Don't be such a spoilsport."

He refrained from further comment as she lowered herself to the ground. She hugged her knees to her chest, and he sat behind her, wrapping his arms around her so that her back was against his front, her hips cradled between his thighs.

She leaned her head back against his shoulder and sighed contentedly.

"Don't you dare fall asleep," he growled.

She laughed. "I'm not going to fall asleep. I'm just relaxing."

He tightened his arms around her. "Maybe this isn't so bad."

"It hasn't really started yet."

"I didn't mean the sunrise," he said. "I meant being here with you. I like the way you fit into my arms."

"I like being in your arms," she admitted.

"You could have been in my arms without leaving the bedroom."

She laughed again. "Just watch the sky."

So he did. They sat together, silent and content, as the sun peeked over the horizon, a spill of brilliant color that spread over the dark canvas until it had obliterated the black and night became day.

It was an awakening of the earth and all its creatures, and Richard was now very much awake.

He lowered his head and pressed his lips to the base of Jenny's throat. She sighed softly. He could smell her shampoo, and the subtle essence of her skin warmed by the early-morning sun. It was a scent that was enticing, arousing and uniquely Jenny.

He pushed the neck of her shirt aside to trail his lips over the ridge of her collarbone as his hands moved beneath the fabric to skim up her sides. He found the clasp at the front of her bra, opened it. The silky weight of her breasts filled his palms.

She moaned when his thumbs scraped over her nipples. "I didn't think you were a morning person."

"You've changed my mind."

"We could, uh, go back to the cabin."

His teeth closed gently over her earlobe. "How isolated are we out here?"

"The nearest neighbors are—" she gasped as his hands continued to tease and his lips nibbled "—miles away."

"We're completely alone?" He shifted to lower her to the ground, his fingers nimbly working the buttons down the front of her shirt.

"Completely," she agreed.

He lowered his head to take one breast in his mouth.

She gasped again as he suckled; moaned again when his hand slid beneath her skirt and between her legs. She was ready for him, and he was hard with wanting her.

He couldn't see the cabin from here. In fact, he couldn't see anything but the lake and the trees and the sun rising over the mountain. It was a place far removed from the world he knew—untouched, uncivilized, untamed. And it stirred within him the most primitive of urges—to mate, to claim, to possess.

Jenny seemed to be driven by the same basic needs. She was as frantic as he was now, as she pushed his shorts over his hips. Her fingers wrapped around him, teasing him, guiding him. As she took him inside, surrounding him with slick heat, something inside him snapped so that even the illusion of control was shattered.

He plunged deep, again and again, in a frenzied pace that she eagerly matched. On the soft emerald grass, under the brilliance of the morning sun, they made love frantically, passionately, recklessly.

He didn't realize how recklessly until he'd emptied himself into her.

He swore softly as he rolled off of her. "I forgot protection."

Jenny reached for her shirt. "Is that something you've done before?" she asked hesitantly.

"No," he told her. He wasn't in the habit of having unprotected sex. In fact, since his divorce, he'd never been with a woman without the protective barrier of a condom between them. "The only concern is pregnancy."

Which was a big enough worry. And if she got pregnant, he knew it would be his fault. Dammit—he knew better than to take such chances. At least he always had before. But in the moment, he'd thought of nothing but his need for her, and now they both might have to face the consequences.

Jenny watched the play of emotions across his face. Panic, frustration, resignation. She knew he was the kind of man who would insist on being there for his child—even if the child was unplanned and unwanted. Thankfully, she took her own precautions. The last thing she wanted was a man tied to her for all the wrong reasons.

"Then there's nothing to worry about, Richard."

"How can you be sure?"

"Because I'm on birth control," she said softly.

"Oh." He exhaled, obviously relieved.

"I got carried away in the moment, too," she admitted. "But I wouldn't risk bringing an unwanted child into this world."

"Unplanned doesn't always mean unwanted," he said gently.

"Maybe not," she agreed. "But as much as I want children someday, I wouldn't let any baby of mine ever think it was a mistake."

"I still owe you an apology."

She shook her head. "We're both equally to blame."

"I just don't want you to think that I'm in the habit of overlooking something so basic."

She managed a smile. "I think your immediate reaction proved otherwise."

Richard sighed. "I've never wanted anyone the way I want you."

"You don't sound happy about it."

"It scares me, that I could need you so desperately I would forget about everything else."

Her heart warmed at this reluctant admission.

"And it scares me," he continued, "that you want things I can't give you. I'm not in a position to think about marriage or a family."

Some of the warmth dissipated now, but she asked lightly, "Have I asked you for any of those things?"

"No. But I know you want them."

She nodded. "But I don't expect them from you. I knew from the beginning that our relationship would have boundaries—I accepted those the night I went back to your hotel room."

"Maybe that's what bothers me," he said. "You deserve more."

"And some day I'll have more," she said. "For now, I only want to be with you."

Although the drive back to Tokyo was filled with easy conversation and comfortable silences, Jenny's heart grew heavier with each mile. She always regretted having to leave the cabin, but her disappointment was even stronger this time because she knew that when they reached the city, the magic of her weekend with Richard would be gone.

She parked in her usual spot beneath the hotel. It was a reasonable walk—or a short subway ride—to her apartment, and it was a lot cheaper to keep her car here than to pay the premium for a parking space closer to her residence.

While they were at the lake, neither had broached the topic of what would happen when the weekend was over. As Jenny unlocked the trunk, she felt awkward wondering whether it would be more appropriate to say good-night or goodbye.

Before she could decide, Richard spoke.

"Will you stay here with me tonight?"

She hadn't anticipated the question, and though she was pleased that he'd asked—grateful to know that he was as reluctant as she to let the weekend end—she knew she should say no. She should go back to her apartment, to give herself some time and space to think. But even knowing their relationship had no future, she wasn't ready to give him up just yet.

"We both have to work in the morning," she said.

It wasn't a yes or a no but an indication that she was willing to be persuaded.

He hefted his duffel bag onto one shoulder, snaked his

other arm around her waist. "There are a lot of hours yet between now and then."

His smile was slow and sexy, filled with promises she knew he could fulfill. She felt her insides quiver.

It terrified her, this reaction to him. He didn't even have to touch her. All it took was a glance, maybe just the hint of a smile, and she was overwhelmed with need for him.

It had never been like this for her before—so completely all-encompassing. She'd never needed anyone as she needed him.

No—she shook off the thought. It wasn't Richard. It was just the newness of their relationship, the fresh blush of desire finally realized.

But even as her mind struggled to rationalize her feelings, she knew it wasn't true. Because she'd been in relationships before—starry-eyed with infatuation and full of confidence for the future.

This was different.

Partly because she already knew there could be no future for her and Richard. Partly because she knew, in her heart, that nothing that had come before compared to what she felt for Richard now. Mostly because she was afraid she would never feel this way again.

Why did she always have to dream the impossible dream? Why couldn't she simply accept what was without wanting more? Why couldn't she enjoy the time she had with Richard now and not worry about what would happen when he was gone?

She had no answers to these questions, no way to soothe the uneasiness in her heart.

It scared her to think how much he'd come to mean to her in such a short amount of time, to realize she was already in danger of falling in love with him. She knew it just as surely as she knew that she would be the one left alone and hurting when he was gone. But that was a problem she could worry about tomorrow.

"I'll stay," she said.

Within minutes they were in his suite, their clothes making a trail from the door to the bedroom.

He'd lost count of the number of times they'd made love since that first momentous occasion Friday night. Every time he thought he was satisfied, desire stirred anew. Then desire would give way to demand. It was as if he couldn't get enough of her. No matter how many times he had her, he wanted her more.

He wanted her now.

He forced himself to take it slowly, exploring every inch of her body, lingering where he knew it pleased her, reveling in the sound of her soft sighs and moans.

He made his way down the length of her body, exploring her with his hands, his lips, his tongue. He paused at her hip, touched the small heart-shaped mark. "Is this a tattoo?"

"No." She laughed softly. "Just a birthmark."

"I like it." He lowered his head and pressed his lips to the spot, then traced the outline with his tongue.

She squirmed, the instinctive movement arousing him beyond belief. He gripped her hips, holding her still while his mouth moved lower. He heard her suck in a breath as his tongue flicked over her, then a gasp as he brought her to the brink of climax, and a long, throaty moan as he pushed her over the edge.

Monday morning, Richard got an extra key card from the front desk for Jenny. He didn't know how long he was going to be tied up in meetings during the day, and he liked the idea of her being there when he got back to his room. He wanted to spend every minute that he could with her.

It was almost eight o'clock when he got in Tuesday night, and she was there as she had been the night before, sitting at the desk, her fingers clicking away on the keys of her laptop. The sight of her tugged at something inside him.

She glanced up when he entered, her lips curving. "Hi."

He dropped his briefcase inside the door and crossed over to her. "Hi, yourself." Then he bent his head to kiss her, long and lingering.

He pushed the chair away from the desk and drew her to her feet, all without taking his lips from hers. She came into his arms willingly, her body melting against his. He knew he could have her naked in his bed in about thirty seconds flat, but he was learning to draw out the pleasure of just being with her and enjoying every minute.

When he finally eased his lips from hers he asked, deliberately casual, "How was your day?"

She tipped her head against his chest and sighed. "Well, it could have been worse."

"What happened?"

"I ran into my sister-in-law in the lobby."

He was silent, waiting for her to elaborate, because so far he wasn't seeing the problem.

"At 7:00 a.m."

"Oh."

She nodded.

"What was she doing here at that hour?"

"John forgot some kind of report or something at home, and she came by to drop it off."

He massaged her shoulders gently, loosening the tight muscles. "Are you worried that she'll tell your brother?"

"I'm twenty-five years old, Richard. I hardly need his permission to sleep with you."

But the tension in her shoulders told a different story.

"And anyway, I don't think Mich will go running to tell him."

"But the possibility concerns you," he guessed.

She hesitated. "I'm just worried that my family will think our being together means something."

He had no right to take offense at her words, but he couldn't deny that her casual dismissal of what was between them bothered him. He dropped his hands from her shoulders and took a step back. "And of course it doesn't mean anything, right?"

"I just don't want my mother thinking about wedding bells when we both know we don't have a future together."

Frustration tangled with the hurt and anger. "Why do you keep bringing up the end of our relationship as if it's a foregone conclusion?"

"Because you'll be going back to Chicago when the negotiations are finished."

He didn't know why he was pushing her. He should be grateful she'd accepted the parameters of their relationship. Instead he said, "Neither one of us can predict the future."

Jenny moved to wrap her arms around him. "I know, and I don't want to waste the time we do have together arguing about this."

"Okay," he agreed. "Let's argue about something else."

She exhaled wearily. "Obviously you have something specific on your mind."

He nodded. "Why do you sneak out of here at 7:00 a.m.?"

This time she stepped away. "I don't sneak."

He wasn't going to debate semantics. "It doesn't make sense that you have to get up an extra hour early every morning to go home and change before work."

"I can hardly wear the same clothes as the day before," she pointed out logically.

"You're deliberately missing my point."

"I just don't see why it should matter to you."

"It matters because I can think of more productive ways to spend the time than on the subway."

"I don't mind."

Maybe she didn't, but he sure as hell did.

She'd told him from the beginning that she didn't do casual relationships. For the past several years, he hadn't been capable of anything more. But he'd pursued her anyway, selfishly and relentlessly, and he'd got what he wanted.

Except that suddenly he wanted more.

"Why don't you want to bring any of your stuff here?"

She hesitated, just a second, before responding. "I don't want to take anything for granted."

"Or is it that you don't want me to take anything for granted?"

"We both know this relationship is only temporary."

And so their disagreement had come full circle again.

He sighed, accepting that he wasn't going to be able to change her mind about a point he'd made so clearly from the start. Instead he said, "If we only have a few weeks together, I want to spend every minute I possibly can with you."

She hesitated a moment before nodding. "I'll go home after work tomorrow to pick up a few things."

"Thank you." He brushed his lips over hers again. "I could meet you at your apartment, make dinner for you."

"Are you growing bored with the hotel menu?" she asked.

"Maybe I just want to cook for you."

"That's an offer I won't refuse," she told him.

Jenny was surveying the contents of her closet, trying to decide which clothes she should take to the hotel. Nerves skittered inside her belly, not because it mattered what she wore to work the next day but because the idea of moving in with Richard—however temporarily—terrified her.

She hadn't expected so much to change so fast.

Friday morning she'd been firm in her resolve to keep Richard at a distance. Friday night she'd spent the night in his bed, in his arms. Every night since then had been the same.

Now it was Wednesday, she'd left him less than twelve hours earlier, and she was missing him already.

She finally decided on a navy pin-striped skirt and a sleeveless silk blouse. She found matching shoes and threw them into a bag along with her underwear and toiletries.

Pushing the closet door shut, she decided that one outfit was enough. *One day at a time.*

Her heart leaped at the knock on the door, and she chided herself for the reaction. This wasn't high school and she wasn't waiting on her date for the prom. She was a grown woman and it was Richard—there was no reason for her sudden jitters. The pep talk did little to settle the quiver in her belly.

He greeted her as he'd got into the habit of doing, with a long slow kiss that made everything inside her melt into a puddle at her feet. There was no doubt that Richard Warren was a first-rate kisser and she sighed, blissfully, contentedly, as she gave herself up to the mastery of his lips.

Tonight, it was a hands-off kiss as he had a bag of groceries in one hand and a flat, wrapped parcel in the other.

"How did you manage at the market?" she asked, when the kiss finally ended.

"I took Yasushi with me," he admitted. "I could tell he was curious as to where I'd be cooking dinner, but he's too polite to ask."

"I'm curious, too," she told him. "About what's in the package."

"It's a present."

"For me?"

"Yes, for you." He offered it to her. "But you have to let me put this food away before you open it."

She helped him unpack the groceries, her curiosity growing by the minute.

Richard sensed her mounting excitement, as well as her careful restraint. He remembered her surprised pleasure when he'd bought her the oyster shell doll and wondered if no one had ever given her presents just for the fun of it.

"Okay," he said, when he'd closed the fridge door. "Open it."

She tore at the plain brown paper with unbridled enthusiasm, then gasped as the painting was revealed.

"Summer Passion." She murmured the title softly, recognizing it immediately. Then she looked up at him, stunned. "How—"

"I saw the way you looked at it, that night at the gallery, and I knew I had to buy it for you."

"It's—wow—I never expected anything like this."

He grinned. "And I never expected to find you at a loss for words."

"I shouldn't accept this," she said, but her fingers gripped the edge of the frame as if she would never let it go.

"Why not?"

"Because I saw the price tag and—"

"Do you like it, Jenny?" he interrupted to ask patiently.

She sighed. "You know I do."

"Then that's all that matters."

"I was going to buy it," she murmured. "But when I went back the next day, it had a sold tag on it."

"I bought it that night but agreed to let the gallery keep it on display through the weekend."

She frowned. "We weren't even lovers then."

He smiled. "But I knew we would be."

"That was quite an assumption to make."

"I was right," he reminded her.

"And I'm too thrilled to have this painting to be annoyed by your smugness." She tore off the last of the paper and tucked the picture under her arm. "Come on. I know exactly where I'm going to put it."

He followed her to the bedroom. She closed the door behind him, leaned the painting against the wall, then started to peel away her clothes.

He watched, his initial fascination quickly supplanted by growing arousal. She was so incredibly beautiful, stunningly passionate, perfect. Okay, he knew she wasn't actually perfect, but she was perfect to him in all the ways that mattered.

She unclipped her bra and added it to the pile of clothing already on the floor.

He swallowed, hard. "I thought you were going to show me where you wanted to hang the painting."

"I will." She smiled as she tugged him down onto the bed with her. "After I show you how grateful I am."

Jenny gulped down a second cup of coffee as she hastily scanned the financial section of the *Japan Times*. Although it was a competitor of the *Tokyo Tribune* and, therefore, not a newspaper to which she subscribed, it was the morning daily that was provided to guests of the hotel and she justified her reading of it as a way of keeping up-to-date with the stories and style of the other paper.

Richard held out a hand as he joined her at the table, and she automatically handed him the front section. If she'd thought about it, she'd be surprised how quickly they'd established a comfortable morning routine. It was almost as if they'd been together for months instead of just ten days, and it was all too easy for Jenny to envision a life with Richard, a home together.

A few more of her clothes hung in the closet now, her toiletries stood next to his in the bathroom, and the novel she was currently reading sat on the bedside table. But the embroidered insignia on the towels and the meals delivered by room service were constant reminders that this was a hotel rather than a home. They were conveniences that reminded Jenny she didn't belong here—and that she didn't belong with Richard.

With that thought weighing heavy on her mind, she passed the rest of the paper to him. "I have to run or I'm going to be late."

"What's your hurry today?"

"Meeting with my editor." She brushed her lips over his. "I'll see you later."

She escaped from the hotel, chased by the guilty knowledge that she'd deliberately lied to him. She wasn't running to a meeting—she was running away from the feelings she could no longer deny.

She tried to remember that she'd only known him a few weeks, but time seemed irrelevant. The only thing that mattered was the rightness she felt with Richard, the sense of belonging that filled her heart whenever she was in his arms.

It couldn't last—she knew that. And she knew it would end with her heart broken if she wasn't careful. She had to believe that she could still protect her heart. She liked Richard, she had fun with him, but she wasn't in love with him—yet. And she wasn't going to let herself fall in love with him.

Except that every minute they were together, she felt herself sinking in deeper. It was too intense, too everything. And yet it wasn't nearly as much as she wanted it to be.

That was why she had to end it.

Chapter Twelve

While Jenny was rushing off to see her editor, Richard was reviewing the files for his meeting with Helen. Mori Taka had announced a day away from the bargaining table, insisting that he had other pressing business to take care of. Richard wasn't sure if it was a legitimate explanation or a tactical move to demonstrate that he had the upper hand in the negotiations—as if everyone at Hanson wasn't well aware of that fact.

It was that knowledge, as much as the delay, that seemed to dishearten Helen, so Richard had suggested an informal meeting in his room to discuss the situation. Not that they hadn't already discussed everything in the greatest detail, but he knew she needed a distraction.

Inviting her to his suite, however, turned out to be the wrong kind of distraction. He realized his mistake as soon as she excused herself to use the washroom after lunch. Sure enough, she returned a few minutes later, a small smile curving her lips.

"I never imagined you'd have a pink toothbrush," she teased. "Or is the green one yours?"

"They're both mine—I'm fastidious about oral hygiene."

Her smile widened. "You know, for a lawyer, you don't lie very well."

"Thank you," Richard said dryly.

"There's that dinner tomorrow night," she reminded him. "Why don't you bring Jenny?"

He'd already planned to invite her, but now he reconsidered. "Why—so you can interrogate her directly?"

"So I can meet her," his boss corrected.

"Why?" he asked again.

"Because I've never known you to be so completely captivated by a woman."

He frowned but couldn't deny the truth of her statement.

"Oh, my," Helen said softly. "You really are serious about her."

"No." But his denial was too quick, almost desperate.

Her smile was sympathetic. "You don't want to be, but you are."

She was right, of course—especially the part about him not wanting to be serious. He'd thought he had everything he wanted: professional respect and financial security—the hallmarks of a successful career he'd dedicated nine years to building. Most importantly, he was content. Or he had been until Jenny Anderson came into his life.

Now he'd found a woman he looked forward to seeing every day. A woman he wanted to fall asleep beside every night and wake up with every morning. A woman who made him think about the future.

He was still thinking about Jenny after Helen had gone. Maybe it was because she'd been on his mind that he wasn't surprised when she walked through the door.

He could tell, though, that she was startled by his presence.

She glanced at the pile of papers on the desk in front of him. "I thought you'd be at TAKA," she said. "I didn't want to interrupt."

"I gave you a key card so you could come and go as you wanted," he reminded her. "And I'm glad you're here because it turns out that I'm finished for the day, and I was hoping I could talk you into playing hooky with me."

"I can't." That was her response—abrupt and final with no further explanation.

He noticed that she'd made her way to the other side of the room, and he suddenly suspected the distance she was establishing wasn't only physical.

"Are you going to tell me why you came back then?"

"I've been doing a lot of thinking," she told him. "And I realized that I can't do this anymore."

He felt his chest tighten. "Do what?"

"Be with you."

The tightness increased. "You didn't seem to have any objections last night. Or this morning."

She looked away, her cheeks flushing. "If it was just sex, there wouldn't be a problem."

"What is the problem?"

"Can't you just accept that I don't want to maintain this charade of a relationship any longer?"

The words were deliberately hurtful, but Jenny was not

a cruel person. It was this knowledge that made him realize there was more going on than she was admitting to.

"No," he said simply.

"No?" she echoed, clearly not having anticipated his objection.

"I'm not going to let you ruin a good thing without at least explaining why."

She crossed her arms over her chest. "I don't owe you any explanations."

"If you don't want to talk about us, why are you here?"

She remained stubbornly silent.

"You came to pick up your things," he guessed.

"Yes, I did." She lifted her chin defiantly and moved past him into the bedroom.

He followed, leaning against the doorjamb as he watched her gather up her belongings, hoping his nonchalant pose would mask the growing uneasiness in his gut. "Why?" he asked again.

"Do we really need to catalog the reasons?"

"I think so," he said, proving his stubbornness could match hers.

Her weary sigh made him want to take her in his arms and comfort her, but he knew she wouldn't welcome any overtures right now.

"I warned you from the start that I don't do casual relationships," she said.

"We've gone way beyond casual. You know how much I care about you, Jenny."

She laughed shortly. "You care about me and I'm already halfway in love with you."

He was still puzzled. "Why is that a problem?"

She moved into the bathroom to retrieve her toothbrush,

shampoo and the scented cream she rubbed on her skin after a shower. "Because I've been through it enough times to recognize the signs, and I can't do it again."

She started toward the door.

"Whoa. Wait a minute." He stepped in front of her. "You're walking away now because you don't want to fall in love with me, is that what you're saying?"

She nodded. "I won't let my heart be broken again."

"That's the stupidest thing I've ever heard."

Her chin came up, her eyes narrowed. "No—stupid was ever getting involved with a man who can't be what I need."

"We both knew the situation from the beginning. Nothing has changed."

"Maybe not for you," she said. "For me, everything has."

For him, too, although he didn't fully realize it until she'd walked out the door.

It had been a difficult but necessary decision for Jenny to make, as she tried to explain to Samara as they were on their way to work the next morning. Her roommate's response wasn't at all what she expected.

"You're an idiot," she said bluntly.

"Thanks for your support."

"Anyone with eyes can tell the man is hung up on you."

"I don't think Richard Warren gets hung up," Jenny denied.

Samara shook her head. "He has major feelings for you and he isn't going to let you go that easily."

"He already did."

"You just caught him off guard. Once he's had a chance to think about it, he'll be back."

This time it was Jenny who shook her head, remembering what he'd once said about not chasing women who weren't interested. Besides, he was tied up now with the merger, too busy finalizing the details to worry about sleeping alone, and probably already looking forward to finishing up his part of the process so he could go back to Chicago.

Except that when she walked into the newsroom and saw the huge bouquet of flowers on her desk, her heart did a funny little flip inside her chest. She wouldn't have thought Richard was the kind of man to make grand romantic gestures, and the initial surge of pleasure was quickly replaced by apprehension.

"I think this proves my tip," Samara said.

"Point," Jenny said automatically, although she wasn't sure it did.

She couldn't imagine Richard choosing such an elaborate and obviously pricey display of roses and lilies and orchids. He would be more likely to show up with a bunch of daisies in hand. But that was the biggest clue—if Richard wanted to give her flowers, he would be there. He wouldn't expect a bouquet—no matter how stunning—to make his case for him.

Jenny pulled the card out of the display.

"Well?" Samara demanded impatiently. "What does it say?"

Jenny stared at the message, at the confirmation of what she'd already known. "They're not from Richard."

Her friend frowned. "Then who—"

"Surprise."

The flowers were a surprise. The presence of Jenny's ex was a shock. Even more astonishing was the way Brad smiled, completely charming and supremely confident, before he planted a firm kiss on her mouth.

"Hey, babe."

Jenny could only stare, baffled and speechless.

Hey, babe. As if she'd been expecting him. As if they'd never even broken up.

She carefully disengaged herself from Brad's embrace and stepped behind her desk.

Samara, who had met Brad only once but had never been a fan of his or his relationship with her friend, had already disappeared. Jenny knew she would face a barrage of questions later, but for now she'd been left alone to face her ex-boyfriend.

"What are you doing in Tokyo?" she asked him.

"I came to see you."

"Why?"

His smile never faltered. "Because I missed you."

She shook her head. She couldn't believe this was happening to her. Not now when she'd finally taken steps to move forward with her life without him, when she'd been on the verge of falling in love with yet another unsuitable man and was still feeling raw about the end of that relationship. "You can't just show up here after more than six months and expect to pick up where we left off."

He walked around the desk, breaching the physical barrier she'd deliberately placed between them. "I spent a lot of time during those six months thinking about you."

"And I spent those six months getting over you."

For the first time, his supreme self-confidence seemed to waver. "You don't mean that, Jenny."

"Yes, I do."

"We've got three years of history together," he reminded her.

"Two and a half years that became history more than six months ago."

Her phone buzzed and Jenny reached for it eagerly. Any interruption was a welcome one right now.

"Richard Warren is here to see you," Kari said.

Almost any interruption, she amended.

"Should I send him in?"

"No, I'll be right there," Jenny said to the receptionist. She didn't know why Richard was here, but she had no intention of introducing him to Brad—especially when she still had no satisfactory explanation for his being in Tokyo right now.

"I'll be back in a minute," she told him.

"I'll be waiting."

As she made her way to the front lobby, she was struck by the irony of the fact that Richard—a frequent visitor to the newsroom over the past couple of weeks—had been stopped at the desk while Brad—a stranger—had walked right in. The difference, of course, was that Brad had a media pass, and the combination of his press credentials and his glib charm would get him in almost anywhere.

All thoughts of her ex dissipated as soon as she saw Richard. Her heart ached, yearned, but she forced a cool smile. "Hi."

His only response to her greeting was to say, "I've got five minutes before I need to get back to my meeting."

"Okay." She didn't know what else he expected her to say.

He took her arm to lead her away from the reception desk and Kari, who was blatantly eavesdropping on their conversation. If the few stilted words they'd exchanged could even be considered a conversation.

There was a definite sizzle in the air when he touched her. Obviously the sexual attraction was still there, no matter how much she might want to pretend otherwise.

He dropped her arm and took a couple of steps away, then came back to her again. He dragged a hand through his hair. She thought he looked tired—or maybe she was just imagining it. Because she'd spent a mostly sleepless night without him was no reason to suspect he'd done the same.

"I can't say everything I need to in five minutes," he finally told her. "There's a dinner tonight at Okumura. Mr. Taka's hosting so I can't get out of it, but you could come with me."

She shook her head. "I can't. I meant what I said—"

"The food is supposed to be first-rate and—"

"You know it's not the menu I have a problem with," she interrupted him this time.

"You blindsided me yesterday," he said quietly.

And she'd hurt him. She could see that now and she regretted it, but it only confirmed that she'd done the right thing in ending the relationship before either of them got any more involved. "I'm sorry for that."

"But not sorry for what you said," he guessed.

She shook her head.

"We need to talk about this."

She started to shake her head again.

"If you won't come to Okumura, I'll come to your place after dinner," he forged ahead, ignoring her protest.

His cell phone rang; he muttered an oath under his breath as he glanced at the display. "I have to go. The meeting's about to resume."

He touched her again, just a brush of his hand over hers, but that simple contact nearly obliterated all of her resolve.

"I'll see you later."

She watched him go, already thinking about what plans she could make for the night ahead. It didn't really matter what she did so long as she wasn't home when Richard stopped by. Because she knew she wasn't strong enough to resist him.

She'd forgotten about Brad until she got back to her desk and found him sitting in her chair, looking as if he had every right to be there. Of course, he probably thought he did.

She bit back a sigh and said, "I have work to do."

He turned the chair so that he was facing her, but didn't move out of it. "Who is he?"

"Who is who?"

"The guy in the lobby."

Her eyes narrowed. "Were you spying on me?"

"Of course not. I just passed by on my way to the men's room."

She pointed to the other side of the newsroom, in the opposite direction from the reception area. "The washrooms are there."

He smiled, shrugged. "I didn't know. I've never been here before."

She wasn't sure she believed his explanation but didn't see any point in making an issue of it. "I really have work to do," she reminded him.

"Okay." He stood up. "What time do you think you'll be finished here?"

"I don't know."

"I'd like to see you tonight, Jenny."

She started to refuse, then hesitated. She didn't want to give Brad any false encouragement, but she wanted to argue with Richard again even less. If she went out with Brad, she wouldn't be home when Richard came to visit, and he would have to accept that she wanted their relationship to be over.

"All right," she said at last.

"Great. We'll pick up something for dinner and go back to your place."

Except the whole point of agreeing to see Brad was so she wouldn't have to face Richard. "I'd rather go out," she told him. "I know a place that—"

"Let me make the plans," he interrupted. "I want to surprise you."

As she watched him go, she wondered why such benevolent words unnerved her.

Jenny's vague sense of foreboding solidified when she figured out where Brad planned to take her for dinner.

"How did you find this restaurant?" she asked.

"I overheard someone talking about it in the newsroom."

Someone—or Richard? Was it possible Brad had overheard Richard inviting her to join him for dinner with the TAKA people?

No, it was a coincidence—an unlikely and unfortunate coincidence—and there was no reason for her to be concerned. It was a big restaurant and still somewhat early for dinner. If she was lucky, she and Brad might be gone before Richard ever arrived.

Still, she hesitated on the sidewalk. "I'm not really that hungry," she said. "Why don't we just go for sushi?"

"Because I'm starving," Brad told her. "And I have a reservation here."

Of course he had a reservation. It was next to impossible to get a table at Okumura without one.

She ignored her discomfort and followed him into the restaurant, inwardly cringing when she saw that the Hanson-TAKA party was already there. The maître d' led them right past the long table where Richard was seated to a smaller, more intimate setting in the corner.

She wondered again if Brad had planned this. But even if he'd somehow known that Mr. Taka had chosen the same restaurant, he couldn't have arranged for them to be dining in such close proximity. Just as Jenny couldn't have guessed that she would feel not just uncomfortable but guilty when her eyes met Richard's across the room.

Dammit, she had no reason to feel guilty. Neither of them had ever made any promises, nor asked for any. It had been casual, easy, temporary. And now it was over.

If she'd had any doubts in that regard, the cold fury in Richard's gaze eliminated them.

Jenny really wasn't hungry, but she dutifully picked at her food, going through the motions without tasting anything. She was conscious of Richard on the other side of the room, of his eyes on her.

She wanted the meal to be over so she could go home. It had been her intention to stay out late, to ensure she wouldn't be there when Richard stopped by. But she knew now that he wouldn't be coming anywhere near her apartment tonight.

"Did you want dessert?" Brad asked.

She shook her head and set her napkin back on the table. "I couldn't eat another bite."

He frowned. "You barely touched your dinner."

"I told you I wasn't very hungry."

He seemed about to say something else, apparently changed her mind. "How about another glass of wine?"

She shook her head again. "No, thanks. I really just want to go."

Annoyance flickered in his eyes. "What's the hurry?"

"It's been a long day, and I'm tired."

"It's barely nine o'clock," he pointed out. "And I brought you here because there's something important I wanted to talk to you about."

She didn't want to talk—she just wanted to go home and cry the tears she'd been holding back since she'd walked out of Richard's hotel room the previous afternoon. But there was one question she felt compelled to ask. "Did you know that Mr. Taka was bringing the Hanson people here?"

His hesitation answered her question before he spoke, "Maybe I did. Maybe I'm not happy about the way a certain lawyer from Chicago has been sniffing around you."

"How do you know anything about Richard Warren?"

"It's my business to find the story," he reminded her. "When I saw you with him this morning, I made a point of asking some questions."

His audacity might annoy her, but it didn't surprise her. Giving Brad the smallest bit of information was like giving a starving dog the scent of a meaty bone.

"Did you get the answers you wanted?" she asked coolly.

"All but one."

"Which one?"

He pinned her with his gaze. "Have you slept with him?"

"I guess I should be grateful you're asking me rather than polling the newsroom."

"Have you?" he asked again.

She couldn't lie to him. She didn't want to lie to him. "Yes."

His mouth thinned. "I can't say I'm happy about that."

"Do you expect me to believe you haven't been with anyone else in the past six months?"

"There have been other women," he admitted. "But only because I was trying to forget about you."

Women—plural. And he was all bent out of shape because she'd been with one other man.

He took her hand again. "It didn't work. I couldn't stop thinking about you, missing you."

"And yet it took you six months to contact me."

"You know me, Jen. I pride myself on my independence. I didn't want to admit that I needed you." He reached across the table for the hand that was resting on the base of her wine glass. "Did you know that I haven't been back to New York for more than a few days at a time since you left?"

"Your six-week assignment lasted six months?"

"I was finished on schedule," he said. "But when I got home, it didn't feel like home anymore. Without you, it was just an empty apartment. So I took another assignment. And another after that. Until I realized, consciously or not, I'd been making my way toward Tokyo."

She remained silent, not sure what kind of response was appropriate.

"But I knew if I came to see you, if I hoped to convince you of my feelings, I couldn't show up empty-handed." He pulled a cellophane-wrapped fortune cookie out of his pocket. "So I brought this for you."

"From China?"

He frowned, obviously missing the subtlety of her point. "From London, actually. I know a guy there who owns a company that makes these." He set the it down in front of her. "Open it."

She opened the wrapper, wondering what kind of fortune he'd dreamed up for her and wishing he hadn't bothered. But she broke open the cookie, then stared speechless at the ring that fell out.

Chapter Thirteen

Jenny thought she'd been shocked when she'd seen Brad in the newsroom, but that moment of incredulity didn't begin to compare to this.

"I want you to marry me," he said.

She didn't know what to say.

She'd never expected, after so many months apart, that he would want not just to reconcile but to move their relationship forward—to take that next final step he'd always seemed so wary of. To offer her everything she'd always wanted.

And it was everything she wanted.

So why wasn't she leaping out of her chair to throw herself into his arms? And why was she now, as he was sliding the ring onto her finger, fighting the urge to pull her hand away?

She knew the answer to all of those questions was the same. Richard.

She heard the scrape of chairs and glanced up as the Hanson-TAKA group started to move toward the door. Richard's mouth was set in a thin line as his gaze moved toward her, disappointment evident in his eyes.

What had she expected—that he would pull her into his arms and beg her to marry him instead of Brad? Yeah, that was as likely as the Yomiuri Giants winning the World Series.

She turned her attention back to Brad and realized that he'd been watching her watch Richard. She felt a twinge of embarrassment, but she refused to feel guilty for having moved on with her life during the time she and Brad had been apart. And she had moved on. She didn't want Brad anymore, she wanted Richard.

How could she possibly accept what Brad was offering when her heart was still aching for Richard?

"I was thinking a fall wedding would be nice," Brad continued.

"This fall?"

"Of course," he said. "We've been apart for too long already."

He was saying the right things, but she knew the real reason he wanted to marry quickly wasn't that he'd missed her so much. She stared at the dazzling marquise diamond on her hand for a moment, then looked up at him.

"Were you even going to tell me about TCR?" she asked softly, referring to the company she knew he'd invested in heavily—a company that had recently declared bankruptcy.

She saw the flicker of surprise on his face, the shadow of guilt in his eyes.

"What does that have to do with anything?" he demanded, a trifle defensively.

"I'm guessing everything."

He frowned. "I love you, Jenny."

"And yet, during the whole two-and-a-half years we were together, living in the same apartment, you never once voluntarily mentioned the word marriage."

"I wasn't ready."

"You're not ready now," she said.

She'd loved Brad once, had even dreamed of marrying him. But all she could think about now was Richard. How her heart had raced when Richard touched her. How her mind had spun when Richard kissed her. How her body had tingled when she'd made love with Richard.

She pulled the ring off her finger. "I can't accept this."

"I thought this was what you wanted."

"A year ago it was," she agreed.

He frowned. "Are you saying no?"

"Yes," she said, with absolutely zero regret. "I'm saying no."

Richard knew the man he'd seen Jenny having dinner with was her ex-boyfriend, but not because she'd told him of her plans. No, during their brief conversation earlier that day, she hadn't even bothered to mention that he was in town. He only knew about Brad because he'd happened to cross paths with Samara as he was leaving the *Tribune* building. She'd been happy to tell him about the unexpected and unwelcome visitor.

But while Samara obviously didn't like her friend's ex, it was Jenny's feelings that mattered. Richard figured the ring on her finger made those feelings pretty clear.

He told himself it shouldn't bother him so much. She'd been honest from the start about wanting a husband and a family, just as he'd been honest about not being the man to give her those things. He should be happy that she was finally getting what she wanted.

Instead, he was selfish enough to be miserable.

Just when he'd started thinking about how they could maintain a relationship after the Hanson-TAKA merger was finalized, his hopes had come crumbling down around him. Even before the ex-boyfriend returned, Jenny had left him, and any hope he might have had of changing her mind had been obliterated by Brad's proposal.

Richard had once worried about her vulnerability. It turned out the joke was on him. She was the one who'd walked out. He knew it hadn't been an easy decision for her to make, but she'd done so anyway, and he'd been the one left with his heart torn open.

Or maybe it was his pride that was in tatters, only his ego that was wounded by her easy dismissal of him and everything they'd shared.

In any case, he had other things to think about. Now more than ever, he wanted this damn merger finalized so he could go back to Chicago and forget he'd ever met Jenny Anderson.

He popped the locks on his briefcase and pulled out Hanson's latest financial reports, determined to put her out of his mind and focus on his work. But the letters and numbers blurred before his eyes and his mind insisted on wandering.

He pushed away from the desk and moved to the window to look out at the street below, his father's words coming back to him again.

And if the woman you love loves you back—

He severed the thought with a laugh that reflected more derision than humor.

Jenny claimed she'd ended their relationship because she was falling in love with him. Following that same logic, he figured she must be completely head-over-heels for him now. It was the only reason he could think of for her to marry another man.

Keiko Irene Anderson came into the world at 10:37 p.m.— a seven-pound fifteen-ounce bundle of wrinkly red skin and spiky black hair with a very healthy set of lungs.

When Jenny finally left the hospital, after cooing over the latest addition to the family and taking her turn to hold her brand-new niece in her arms, she intended to go home. She needed to think, to process everything that had happened in the past twenty-four hours, and she needed to sleep.

But instead of going home, she found herself in front of the hotel. Had she planned to come here all along?

She didn't know. But now that she was here, she knew she couldn't leave without seeing Richard.

Still, nerves skipped in her tummy as she made her way to the elevator, up to the twenty-second floor, then down the corridor. The last time she'd come had been to tell him that their relationship—barely begun—was over. She hadn't expected that she'd have reason to come back to the hotel while Richard was still here. And she wasn't sure it was reason so much as need that had compelled her to come now.

She just wanted to explain about Brad. She could only imagine what he thought, knowing she'd been in his bed only days before receiving a proposal from another man. And she thought he might want to know about the baby.

Or maybe she was just making excuses.

She ignored this niggling thought as easily as the Do

Not Disturb sign hanging on the handle and rapped her knuckles against the wood.

She waited a minute, maybe two, and had lifted her hand to knock again when the door was yanked open.

"You're the absolute last person I expected to see tonight," Richard said to her.

She twisted the strap of her purse around her hand, suddenly aware that she had no idea what time it was. She didn't know when she'd left the restaurant or how long she'd been at the hospital. Whatever the hour, Richard clearly hadn't been sleeping.

He was still dressed in the suit he'd been wearing at dinner, although the jacket had been discarded and the tie loosened. His hair looked slightly rumpled, as if he'd run his hands through it. His jaw was shadowed with stubble and his eyes were dark. He looked sexily disheveled and just a little bit dangerous.

That thought gave her pause. *Dangerous* wasn't a word she would ever have associated with him before. Then again, he'd never looked at her quite this way before.

She ignored the quiver of nerves to ask, "Can I come in?"

His only response was to step back to allow her entry.

He closed the door behind her, then moved across the room to pick up a glass of amber liquid. She guessed it was probably the whiskey that was responsible for the edgy glint in his eyes.

"You're not wearing his ring," he noted, lifting the glass to his lips as she stepped past him.

"I—" she cleared her throat "—no."

"Did you turn down his proposal?"

She wished he'd offer her a drink or invite her to sit down—anything to ease this uncomfortable situation.

But he did neither, merely standing across the room watching her.

"Yes."

He seemed surprised by her response, but quickly recovered to ask, "Why? I thought you wanted to get married and have a family. Isn't that, after all, why you dumped me?"

She winced at the anger in his tone. "My decision to end things with you had nothing to do with Brad. It still doesn't."

"Because what we had between us would never have been enough for you."

He was right. What they'd shared together, as wonderful as it had been, wouldn't have been enough. She would eventually, inevitably, have wanted more. She knew herself well enough to have anticipated that, and she knew Richard well enough to know that he couldn't give her what she needed. It was the reason she'd ended their relationship.

I care about you, Jenny.

The memory of his words evoked both joy and pain. Joy because she knew that he did care; pain because caring wasn't loving. And she'd promised herself that she would never settle for second best again.

But she couldn't deny that she missed him. She felt the tightness in her throat, the threat of tears she hadn't yet let herself shed. "I'm not sure what I want anymore," she admitted.

"Then why are you here?" he asked again, more gently this time.

"I, ah, came to tell you that that Michiko had her baby. Another girl." She smiled. "Keiko."

"When?"

"Tonight. She's beautiful." Jenny smiled. "She wasn't

an hour old when I got to hold her in my arms—this brand-new baby, a tiny perfect human being."

She could still feel the slight weight of the fragile bundle in her arms and the pang of longing so deep inside it made her want to cry.

"I do know what I want," she said.

"A baby," he guessed.

"A family," she corrected. "All my life, I've never quite felt as though I fit. I love my parents and John and Michiko and their beautiful little girls, but I've always felt a little disconnected—as if they'd been given to me to share but weren't really mine. I want a family of my own."

It was a dream he'd once had, too. But that dream had faded a long time ago. His father's death had been the first blow, a hard lesson in the fragility of life; his mother's abandonment had confirmed the capriciousness of love; finding his wife with another man had only solidified his doubts and questions. No, a family wasn't something he'd dared dream about in a long time.

Except when he'd been with Jenny, then he'd found himself wanting more than he should. He'd found himself thinking about a future with her in it. Even as he'd reminded himself it was a fantasy—a dream that could never be reality because her life was here and his was in Chicago—he'd convinced himself the obstacle of distance wasn't insurmountable if they both wanted to be together.

Of course, her dumping him effectively destroyed those illusions.

"If you want a family of your own so much, why didn't you accept Brad's proposal?"

She didn't answer.

"Okay," he said when she remained silent. "Why don't you tell me why you're really here?"

"Obviously I made a mistake." She started toward the door.

He grabbed her arm and turned her around to face him again. "Did you come to see if I'd be willing to make the same offer? How far are you willing to go to entice me?"

His lips hovered above hers. He saw her eyes widen, felt the soft exhale of her breath. He pressed his body against hers, let her feel his arousal. As angry as he was with her, as frustrated as he was with the situation, he couldn't deny that she still turned him on. And having her back in his arms, even like this, aroused him beyond belief.

Apparently he wasn't the only one affected by their nearness. Jenny moaned as she shifted instinctively, cradling the ache of his arousal between the softness of her thighs.

He bit back a groan of frustration as he tried to remember that she'd dumped him, trampled right over his heart on her way out the door. But right now, with her back in his arms, he didn't seem to care. Or maybe he cared too much.

He crushed his mouth down on hers. He was furious and frustrated and hurting more than he was willing to admit, and all of that pent-up emotion poured into the kiss.

He expected her to slap him—he deserved to be slapped. At the very least, he expected that she would pull away. Instead she moaned, her lips parting for the ruthless on-slaught of his tongue. Her hands weren't pushing against him but holding on, her fingers curled into the fabric of his shirt. Her body molded to his, soft curves yielding to hard angles, her heart beating in frantic rhythm against his.

Somehow, without either of them being aware, anger gave way to ardor and passion transformed to tenderness.

She trembled. Or maybe he did.

He was no longer certain where she left off and he began; it no longer mattered. The taste of her seeped into his blood, more potent than any whiskey. His hands moved over her body, no longer punishing and demanding but seeking and giving.

His lips skimmed over her cheeks, tasted the saltiness of her tears. Whatever point he'd intended to make was lost in the realization that he'd hurt her, and that was the one thing he'd never wanted to do. He leaned his forehead against hers. His voice, when he spoke, was thick with emotion, regret.

"Give us a chance, Jenny."

She brushed the tears off her cheeks, moved toward the door. "I already did."

He had maybe a few seconds before she walked out on him again. A few seconds to find the words that could change the rest of his life. No closing argument he'd ever made before a judge had been so important.

But what could he do? If she'd already made up her mind, what was left to say?

I love you.

The answer seemed obvious, but the words stuck in his throat. He couldn't do it. Even if it was true, he couldn't use those words to manipulate her.

All he said was, "You wouldn't have kissed me the way you just did if this was over."

She looked up at him, her eyes filled with equal parts sadness and determination. "It has to be over."

"Why?" He heard the desperation in his voice, but he was beyond caring.

A single tear trembled on the edge of her lashes before

it spilled over and tracked slowly down her cheek. "Because if I give you a chance, you'll break my heart. And I don't want to hurt anymore."

Richard had tossed back several more glasses of whiskey after Jenny's visit before accepting that no amount of alcohol would cleanse the taste of her lips or banish her image from his mind. Then, when he'd finally crawled into bed and slept, he'd dreamed of her. Dreams in which he'd been able to see her but was unable to reach her. Dreams in which he'd been running toward her while she slowly faded away. He didn't need a psychiatrist to figure out she was lost to him. Not just in his dreams but forever.

When he awoke, he felt as though a jackhammer was pounding into his skull, but even the pain in his head couldn't make him forget the emptiness in his heart. A long shower and a handful of aspirin did nothing to improve his disposition. Though he wasn't in the mood to make pleasant conversation, he had no legitimate excuse to cancel the breakfast meeting Helen had set up the night before and he was at her suite by 8 a.m.

"You look like hell," she said upon opening the door.

Richard moved past her to pour himself a much-needed cup of coffee from the service that had been set up in her sitting area. "I knew I should have gone with the blue tie."

"It would match the circles under your eyes," she agreed.

He swallowed a mouthful of hot coffee. "I was up late."

"Working?"

"What else?"

She refilled her own cup and sat down. "I'm glad I'm not paying you by the hour or we'd be bankrupt already.

Not that I believe for a minute that the merger caused you to lose sleep last night."

"The merger is the only thing that matters right now." He perused the tray of pastries. It was easier to pretend he was hungry than to face the pity in Helen's eyes.

When it became obvious to her that he didn't intend to say anything more, Helen sighed. "I thought we were friends, Richard."

"We are," he agreed.

"Then why won't you tell me what's going on?"

He selected a cherry Danish he didn't really want and set it on a plate. "Because I'm a man, and we don't like to admit our mistakes."

"Then you're admitting you made one?"

He nodded. Although whether his biggest mistake was in ever getting involved with Jenny Anderson or letting her walk out of his hotel room last night, he didn't know. In any event, she'd made it clear that whatever they'd shared was over.

But what choice had he given her? What had he offered other than a few weeks of his life and a good time in his bed? Of course she wanted more. She deserved more.

He didn't want ties, commitments, obligations—and he definitely didn't want to fall in love. What was love anyway but a four-letter excuse for hurting those you claimed to care about?

Marilyn had said she loved him, but that hadn't stopped her from sleeping with another man. Not even parental love was dependable. His father had died and his mother had withdrawn her affection from her elder son. No, he didn't ever intend to put his heart on the line again.

Jenny was better off with someone who wanted the same things she did. Someone who would put her needs first, who would love her and give her the future and family she wanted. But the thought of her with any other man—exchanging vows with him, making love with him—he couldn't let himself think about it. The idea of her in any other man's bed drove him insane.

"Do you think you'll ever get married again?" he asked, surprising himself as much as Helen with the question that tumbled out of his mouth.

A smile played at the corners of her mouth. "Are you proposing?"

"No," he said quickly, then winced at the vehemence of the denial.

She laughed. "It's lucky for you I'm not easily offended."

Richard decided to keep his mouth shut until his brain started functioning normally again.

"I know there's been a lot of speculation—public and private—about my marriage to George. But regardless of what anyone says or thinks, I married him because I loved him.

"Maybe I was idealistic," she admitted. "Maybe even a little naive. But I had hopes and dreams like any young bride when I made my vows."

She shrugged. "Some of those hopes faded, some of my dreams changed. That happens not just in marriage but in life.

"But to answer your question, yes." She smiled, a little wistfully. "If I ever fell in love with someone who could believe in my dreams—I would get married again.

"However, I think the real question you need to answer is—would *you* get married again?"

Richard raked a hand through his hair and sighed. "I don't know."

A month ago, he wouldn't have had any difficulty answering that question with a resounding no. But a month ago, he didn't know Jenny. Now, he couldn't imagine his life without her.

If he had to choose between making a commitment and losing her forever, he would marry her.

But his pride wouldn't let him ask—not now.

He wanted her to choose him not because he was willing to put a ring on her finger, but because she loved him.

As he loved her.

The realization should have come as a shock, maybe even sent him into something of a panic—instead, the acceptance of his feelings filled him with an unexpected warm contentment.

He was scared, too, but as much as he feared putting his heart on the line and having it rejected as both his mother and his ex-wife had done, he was even more afraid of losing Jenny forever.

Chapter Fourteen

Jenny stopped by the hospital to see Mich and the baby on her way home from work the next day. The visit with her sister-in-law and new niece was a bittersweet reminder of the dreams of a family of her own that continued to elude her. She was on her way out when her brother and Suki were coming in.

John left his elder daughter with her mother and baby sister to follow Jenny outside.

"I heard Brad proposed to you," he said.

Jenny didn't bother to ask where he'd heard. Her brother had contacts everywhere in the city. Instead, she nodded.

"Please tell me you're not going to marry him," John said.

"I'm not going to marry him."

He frowned at the immediate response. "Do you mean that or are you just humoring me?"

She smiled. "You don't have a sense of humor."

"Not about something like this," he agreed. "Because I don't want to see you get hurt again."

"I'm old enough to make my own decisions," she reminded him gently. "And to face the consequences of those decisions."

He sighed. "I know, but just because you've grown up doesn't mean I can stop wanting to protect you."

"Old habits die hard?"

"Something like that."

Despite his general agreement, she could tell he had something specific on his mind. And she was sure she knew what it was.

"You found out about TCR, didn't you?"

His startled glance confirmed she was right—somehow her brother had learned that Brad's big investment had turned out to be a big dud.

"I didn't realize you knew about it," he said.

"I'm not an idiot, John. Don't you think I wondered why Brad was suddenly so anxious to marry me?"

"I don't think you're an idiot," he assured her. "But I did think that your history with him might have clouded your judgment."

She just shook her head.

He took her hand, squeezed it affectionately. "I'm glad. You deserve so much better."

She felt her throat tighten, and she knew she had to change the subject quickly before she embarrassed both of them by breaking into tears.

Before she had a chance, however, John spoke again. "I thought for a while, before Brad came into town, that you and Richard Warren—"

"I don't want to talk about Richard," she interrupted.

"I'm sorry," he said gently. "When I saw the two of you together, the way he looked at you, I got the impression he really cared about you."

Which was the same way Richard had described his feelings, but her heart ached for love too much to settle for anything less.

"I didn't get a chance to talk to Suki," she said in an obvious effort to change the topic of conversation. "How's she liking her new sister?"

John's gaze held hers for a long moment before he answered. "I think she's still undecided at this point. She was excited about the idea of a sister, but I don't think Keiko is quite what she had in mind."

"It must be a difficult adjustment for her," Jenny said. "To go from being an only child to being the older sibling of a baby who's getting all the attention."

"Yeah, it is." He grinned at her.

"As if you remember," she scoffed.

"I do." He tugged a strand of her hair playfully. "Actually what I remember most was the way you used to follow me around. Everywhere I went, wanting to do everything I did. It drove me nuts.

"Then you started to grow up, make friends of your own, do your own thing. You hardly paid any attention to me anymore. That's when I realized how much I missed you."

"You missed bossing me around," she teased.

"Yeah, that, too. Although it will take Suki another couple of years to appreciate that benefit of having a little sister."

Jenny shook her head despairingly, but their discussion about Suki had given her an idea.

"Why don't I take Suki to the lake for the weekend?"

she suggested. "It will give you and Mich some time alone with the baby and give Suki some special attention."

"Suki would love that," he agreed.

Jenny was glad she'd suggested coming up to the cabin with her niece. Although she couldn't help being reminded of her last visit with Richard, she was determined not to dwell on it. This had always been her favorite place, and she wasn't going to let recent events ruin the enjoyment for her.

After dinner, she and Suki went for a walk in the woods, then they popped some corn and sat in front of the TV to watch one of Suki's favorite cartoon programs. Jenny loved her niece's company—she was honest and straightforward and uncomplicated.

"I thought it would be fun to have a sister," Suki confided, munching on a handful of popcorn. "But Keiko doesn't do anything except sleep and cry."

She smiled as she stroked a hand over the little girl's silky hair. "That's all you did when you were a baby, too."

Her niece was obviously skeptical. "Really?"

She nodded. "And then you started to crawl and walk and run. And now there's nothing you can't do."

"I can't drive a car," Suki said wisely, reaching into the bowl again. "And I'm not allowed to use Mommy's scissors unless she's helping me."

"That's a good rule," Jenny agreed.

Suki was silent for a few minutes, watching the television, before she asked, "Are you going to have a baby, Aunt Jenny?"

The ache she felt inside was getting to be familiar—a bone deep yearning mixed with too much uncertainty. "I hope so," she said. "Someday."

Suki nodded. "But you've got to get a husband first."

Not technically, but Jenny didn't bother to correct the little girl on that. As she'd told Richard, if she was going to bring a baby into the world, she wanted him or her to have a mother and father who loved one another and were committed to raising their child together.

"If you don't get a husband," Suki continued, "you could borrow me. I could be your little girl sometimes."

She hugged the child closer, touched by her niece's generous heart. "Like we're doing now?"

"Just like this." Suki snuggled into her lap, and within a few minutes, she'd closed her eyes.

Jenny waited until the program was over to make sure the she was completely asleep, then lifted her carefully to carry her to bed. She'd just finished tucking the covers around her when she heard a knock.

She hurried to the door before a repeat of the sound could wake her niece. She'd thought it might be one of the distant neighbors, or somebody who'd gotten lost and needed directions to get back to the highway. It never even crossed her mind that it might be Richard.

He brought his hand from behind his back, offering her a tentative smile along with a bunch of wilting daisies.

The flowers completely disarmed her, because they were exactly what she'd once envisioned he would choose if he were to give her flowers. She accepted the bouquet automatically, her throat tightening as she touched a soft white petal. But she couldn't let Richard know that she weakened so easily, so she continued to stand in the doorway, not inviting him inside. "What are you doing here, Richard?"

"I wanted to apologize for the other night. When you came to my hotel."

She sighed. "There's nothing to apologize for," she told him.

"Then why did you run away?"

"I didn't run away," she denied. "I simply came up here to spend some time alone with my niece."

"I've missed you," he said softly.

She'd barely managed to rebuild some of the walls around her heart, and he was already tearing them down. She wished she were strong enough to turn him away, but she'd missed him, too. She sighed and stepped away from the door. "You can come in for a few minutes."

He followed her into the family room, sat beside her on the sofa, his body turned so he could look at her. "I've been thinking about what you said the other night," he told her. "About wanting a family of your own."

"You don't have to tell me again that you don't want the same thing," she told him.

His fingers stroked down her cheek, a gentle caress. "I didn't think I did," he admitted. "But I've started to realize that wants can change—or maybe it's the people who come into our lives who make us want different things."

She felt her heart leap, but forced her voice to remain calm. "What are you saying?"

He was silent for a long minute before he finally said, "I want to help you find your birth mother."

Okay, that wasn't quite what she had expected.

"I told you before, I'm not interested in looking for a woman who wasn't interested in me."

"How do you know she wasn't interested?" he challenged.

"She gave me away, didn't she?"

"And now you're rejecting her because she rejected you first, and you keep waiting for everyone else to do the same thing." He shook his head. "Actually, you don't wait. You leave so that no one can leave you."

"That's ridiculous."

"Is it? It seems to me that's exactly what happened with us."

"Did you come all this way to psychoanalyze me?"

"No, I came all this way to tell you I love you."

She stared at him, stunned.

He smiled wryly. "I didn't expect it, either."

She pushed herself up from the sofa. "I'm going to have a glass of wine, do you want one?"

He followed her to the kitchen area. "Does that offer mean you're not going to kick me out tonight?"

She shrugged as she took two glasses from the cupboard. "There's a spare bedroom."

He waited patiently while she uncorked the bottle then poured the wine. He accepted the glass she passed to him before asking, "Aren't you going to say anything?"

"My mind is still spinning."

"Mine, too." He set his wine down, then pried hers from her fingers and placed it on the counter beside his own. He took her hands, linking their fingers together. "I didn't think I would ever fall in love again. I know I didn't want to. But you changed everything for me, and I don't ever want to be without you again."

She still didn't say anything, but he felt her fingers tremble slightly in his grasp. He squeezed them gently before he let her go.

"Give me another chance—give *us* another chance, Jenny."

"I haven't kicked you out," she said. Then added, "Yet."

He smiled. "I'm grateful."

"That doesn't mean I'm not thinking about it."

"Of course not."

He was being agreeable again and smiling that smile that made her knees weak. She wanted more than anything to give him another chance—to give *them* another chance. It was because she wanted it so much that she forced herself to take a step back.

She'd been on an emotional roller coaster the past few days and didn't know if she could trust anything she was feeling right now. "I'm too tired to think about this right now. I need to go to bed."

"Okay." He reached for her hand as she started to move past him, halting her in her tracks. "But there's one more thing you need to think about."

Then he lowered his head and pressed his lips to hers.

It was the briefest touch, a test, a taste.

Then his mouth brushed over hers again. She sighed and her eyelids fluttered closed as she tried to remember if he'd ever kissed her like this before—with endless patience and gentle persuasion. The passion was still there, she could feel it simmering just beneath the surface, but there was also tenderness and affection, and a hint of something warmer, softer, deeper. She was just starting to sink into it, allowing herself to be seduced by him, when he eased back.

"Sweet dreams, Jenny."

Richard was awakened to the sound of a steady, rhythmic thump against the wall directly behind his head. He pushed himself up in bed, taking a moment to orient himself in the unfamiliar surroundings.

He was at Jenny's parents' cabin. She hadn't spent the

night with him—which wasn't a surprise but still a disappointment, but she'd let him stay—which was a relief as much as a surprise. He hoped it meant that she hadn't written him off completely. He hadn't expected the declaration of his feelings to break down all the barriers between them, but he hoped it would at least be a step toward building a life for them together.

The continued thumping drew his attention again. He pulled on his clothes and went to investigate.

The door of the room beside his was open, and there was a child on the bottom bunk. She was lying across the narrow mattress, her head hanging over the edge, her feet swinging back and then forward, thumping against the wall.

Well, that explained the noise.

"You must be Suki," he said.

She tumbled off the bed, her face splitting in a wide grin as she nodded enthusiastically. "Auntie Jenny's making breakfast."

"Is that why you woke me up?"

She shook her head, wide-eyed, innocent. "I promised not to wake you and not to go into your room."

Richard couldn't help but smile. "I guess you didn't do that," he agreed. "But now that I'm awake, why don't we go find out what's for breakfast?"

She nodded again, obviously approving his suggestion, and placed her hand inside his much larger one. "I'll show you the kitchen."

Richard had offered to cook dinner for all of them, but after a day of hiking, Suki almost fell asleep at the table before he'd even boiled the water for the pasta. Jenny gave her a bowl of cereal and got her ready for bed.

While the sauce was simmering, he opened a bottle of wine and set the table.

"Looks like you thought of everything," Jenny said when she came back into the room.

He handed her a glass of wine. "I seem to have forgotten candlelight and soft music."

She took a long sip of the merlot. "Candles are a fire hazard and music inhibits conversation."

"Are you really so unromantic?"

"I appreciate romance at the right time and place," she said. "But this isn't it."

"Sometimes you have to make the time and place." He lowered his head to hers and kissed her softly. He felt rather than heard her sigh and though he was tempted to deepen the kiss, he forced himself to pull back. Her eyes were soft, clouded, her lips still slightly parted.

"I've been wanting to do that all day," he told her.

"I've been thinking that I should have sent you back to the city last night."

"You're not going to get rid of me that easily this time," he told her.

"What if I start using words like commitment or marriage and babies?"

"Try me," he said.

She studied him for a moment, then shook her head. "I'm not sure this is a good idea."

"This?" he asked.

"You and me."

"I think it's a very good idea." He dumped the pasta into the pot, set the timer, then came back to where she was standing and kissed her again. "The best idea I've ever had, in fact."

"I should send you back to the city now."

"It's too late."

She sighed. "I know."

But she didn't sound happy about it, so he steered the conversation to more neutral topics as he finished dinner preparations and throughout the meal. They worked together clearing up afterward, and then Jenny went to check on Suki.

"She hasn't moved since I tucked her in," she told him.

He took her hand and led her over to the sofa. "I remember your mother commenting that Suki reminds her of you. I think she's right."

Jenny laughed as she sat down beside him. "The resemblance is uncanny, isn't it?"

"Not that she looks like you, but she has your spirit—your tenacity and endurance. She's a great kid."

"Yes, she is."

"And you're going to be a great mother someday."

"Maybe." Her voice was wistful. "Someday."

He was surprised by how much he wanted to give Jenny the gift of a child, to see her belly grow round with their baby inside it. "How many kids do you want to have?"

"Two or six or a dozen." She smiled, then shrugged. "At least two."

It was easy to imagine her surrounded by children, obvious that she had enough love for twelve of them.

And he knew now that he wanted to give her what she wanted, because he'd finally realized it was what he wanted, too. Not marriage and family in an abstract sense, but to marry Jenny and have children with her. To live with her and grow old with her. To be with her forever.

It was suddenly so clear to him, but he knew she would

need some time to trust he'd changed his mind before they could make those kind of plans. Still, he couldn't help asking, "When you think about the future, do you see me with you?"

"Why are you asking me that question?" She sipped her wine. "Aren't you going back to Chicago in a few weeks?"

"Most likely," he agreed. "There are things I'll need to deal with on that end to get this merger off the ground."

She nodded.

"Any chance you would go with me?"

Her eyes widened. "To Chicago?"

"Just until the details are worked out, then we could come back here."

"You want to come back to Tokyo?"

"I want to be with you, Jenny—whatever that takes."

"Why?" she asked softly, the question tinged with both hope and skepticism.

"Because I love you," he said again. "And I'd like to think that wherever the future takes us, we can find a way to be together."

Again, she sidestepped the declaration of his feelings, shifting so that she was straddling his lap, her knees bracketing his hips. "Let's not worry about tomorrow." She touched her mouth to his, nibbling gently. "Not tonight."

He bit back a groan as she rocked against him. He really wanted to talk to her, to make plans with her, but the sensual movements of her body were making it difficult for him to even think. "Your, uh, niece is sleeping down the hall," he reminded her.

"Suki is a very sound sleeper." She was already tugging his shirt out of his pants, sliding her palms up over his chest.

He loved the coolness of her fingers on his skin, the eagerness of her touch. "That isn't what you said last night."

"Last night I wanted you to suffer—at least a little." She pressed her lips to his chest, swirled her tongue around his nipple. Then she tipped her head back, her lips curving in a seductive smile. "Tonight, I want you to suffer a lot."

Helen was becoming increasingly frustrated by the delays. She was even more frustrated by the realization that she wasn't in any position to make demands. TAKA was in control of every step of the negotiations and then had final say over whether or not the merger would even happen. There was nothing she hated more than being on the weak end of such a power imbalance—it made her feel like she was sixteen years old again, knowing she couldn't have the one thing she wanted more than anything else in the world.

Twenty-five years later, she felt just as helpless. She forced herself to push those feelings aside as she poured another cup of coffee and waited for Richard to arrive.

She forgot about ancient resentments and current concerns when he walked through the door. He looked different—she noticed that right away—more settled, and happier than she'd ever seen him. Definitely happier than the last time they'd had a morning meeting like this.

"Looks like somebody had a good weekend," she said.

"It was a great weekend."

"Then you worked things out with Jenny?"

"Not all the details, but those will come."

She was genuinely pleased for him. With everything else in chaos around her, it was comforting to believe in the healing power of love.

"I'm going to marry her," Richard announced.

Helen had started to lift her cup to her lips, then set it down again. "When you decide to move, it's always full speed ahead. When's the wedding?"

"Soon." He smiled. "Jenny doesn't know yet."

"When are you going to let her in on this plan?"

"Soon," he said again.

"Last time we spoke about marriage, you were reluctant to even consider making that kind of commitment again," she reminded him.

"That was before I fell in love. Now I don't want to imagine ever waking up without her."

Helen's heart sighed at the emotion in his words, and at the same time it ached knowing that she could only dream about being loved so deeply and completely.

"The only thing that scares me now is the thought of the dozen or more children Jenny wants to have," Richard said.

She pushed her own regrets aside to respond to his concern. "I think you'll be a terrific father."

"I hope so," he said. "But you know from your own experience with Jack and Evan and Andrew how much grief kids can give you—and they're not even your own."

She felt the familiar pang and accepted it. "No, they're not."

"I'm sorry," he said. "I didn't mean to sound insensitive."

"You didn't. It's true. I've tried to be their mother, but I'm not." Maybe they might have felt closer to her, opened up more easily, if she'd had George's baby—a tie of blood to join them together—but years of trying had been both unsuccessful and heart-wrenching.

"Did you ever wish you'd had a child of your own?"

She swallowed the regrets, the grief, the guilt, before responding softly, "I did have a child."

His eyes widened, reflecting his shock.

He couldn't be any more surprised than she was. Her child wasn't something she ever talked about, but the baby she'd given up had been on her mind almost constantly since the twenty-fifth anniversary of that date. Maybe it was time she unburdened herself of the secret she'd carried for so long. "A little girl," she admitted softly.

"You've never mentioned having a daughter."

"I was only sixteen when I got pregnant. It seemed the best thing to do—for both of us—was to give her up for adoption."

"I'm sorry, Helen. I know that must have been hard for you."

She nodded. "Hardly a day's gone by since then that I haven't thought about what might have been different if I'd kept her, wondered if giving up my baby was the right decision.

"It was twenty-five years ago on August second," she told him. "And I still remember every detail. I got to hold her in my arms for only a few minutes before they took her away, but I'll never forget the soft downy hair, the perfect little fingers and even tinier fingernails, the heart-shaped birthmark on her hip."

Richard froze. "A birthmark?"

Helen smiled as she blinked the moisture from her eyes. "It wasn't very big. Maybe it wasn't even a heart. But I thought it was. And I told her it was a symbol of my heart that she could carry with her forever, so she would always know she was loved."

He thought back to the bouquet of balloons he'd seen

in Jenny's office—the admission that it had been her twenty-fifth birthday on the second of August. He knew that she had a heart-shaped birthmark on her hip, and now he knew why she always looked so familiar to him.

Jenny was Helen's daughter.

Chapter Fifteen

"I used to believe I'd find her," Helen continued, lost in her memories. "During the first year after my baby was born, I looked into every stroller I passed, searching for the slightest hint of familiarity. I can't count how many times I thought—maybe it's this child, maybe it's her."

"Have you tried to find her?" Richard asked.

"I considered it," she admitted. "But I figured, having given her up once, I had no right to interfere in her life later. I also figured she would have tracked me down if she wanted to."

And she hasn't.

The unspoken words echoed in the silence of the room.

"Do you want to find her?" he asked softly.

"More than anything else in the world. I want to see my little girl again."

"Your little girl is twenty-five years old now," he reminded her gently.

"I know." She managed a tremulous smile. "Objectively I understand that. But despite the passing of time, in my heart, I still think of her as the baby I held so briefly in my arms."

Richard didn't respond. He could hardly tell Helen that her daughter had grown into a beautiful young woman—a woman who had made it clear she had no interest in finding the mother who had given birth to her and given her up.

Jenny was pleasantly surprised when Kari buzzed through to tell her that Richard was there to see her. He came through the newsroom a few minutes later carrying two bento box lunches.

He smiled at her, but she sensed the tension in him.

"I thought you would be tied up in negotiations at TAKA all day," she said.

He set the boxes on her desk. "We seem to alternate between periods of intense negotiation and twiddling our thumbs."

Today he was obviously twiddling his thumbs, and she guessed the inactivity with respect to the merger was responsible for his tension. She knew he was anxious to finalize the deal. Was he also anxious to return to Chicago? Did he still want her to go with him?

He hadn't mentioned the possibility since they'd returned from the lake, and she was wishing now that they'd talked about it more while they were there. But she'd been taken aback by the suggestion, thrilled at this evidence that he wanted their relationship to continue, and equally scared to hope that it could. There were a lot of obstacles to overcome if they were to build a future together and after having her heart broken so many times before, she was almost afraid to let herself believe they could make it work. But she wanted to try. She wanted to be with him.

One day at a time, she reminded herself again.

"I did see my boss this morning, though," Richard told her.

"Did that meeting go well?"

He smiled, but she still saw the hint of shadows in the curve of his lips. "Helen wants to meet you."

"She does?" Jenny was both surprised and a little apprehensive.

"She's curious about the woman who's stolen my heart."

"You didn't tell her that?"

This time when he smiled, it came more naturally. "I didn't have to. She said it was the smile on my face that gave it away."

Jenny felt her cheeks flush as her own lips curved.

"She invited us both to have dinner with her tonight," he said.

"Do you want to?" she asked, sensing there was something about the suggestion that was causing him to hesitate.

"I would really like you to meet Helen," he admitted. "But there's something you need to know before you decide whether or not you want to."

"What's that?"

He paused, cleared his throat. His obvious hesitation made her tummy flutter with apprehension.

"Just tell me," she said.

"During our conversation this morning, Helen mentioned that she had a baby a long time ago, and she gave her up for adoption."

She considered the revelation as the slow, throbbing ache of longing she'd learned to deny so long ago began to beat inside her breast again. Jenny was adopted; Helen had given her baby up for adoption. She wasn't sure if that gave them something in common or set them apart. She guessed Richard was wondering the same thing. "And you think, because I was adopted, I'll hold that against her?"

"I wish it was that simple," he said.

She frowned.

"I think you're Helen's daughter."

Jenny could only stare at him, stunned. Then she shook her head. "That's impossible."

Richard reached across the desk for her hand, but she pushed her chair back and stood up.

"Helen's daughter was born on August second twenty-five years ago," he told her.

She shook her head again. "It's just a coincidence."

"I'm not telling you this to upset you," he said gently. "But I think this could be a great opportunity for you to finally know your biological mother."

She turned away. "I don't want to talk about this. The idea is just too ridiculous."

"I know it seems unlikely—"

"I doubt I'm the only child born on that day who was given up for adoption," she interrupted.

"You're probably right."

The easy agreement and soothing tone didn't help to ease the panic building inside her. Somehow she knew there was more to come.

"And if it was only your age and date of birth, I wouldn't have jumped to any conclusions," he told her.

"What else is there?" she demanded.

"You look like her."

"She's blond," Jenny said automatically.

"Which is probably why I didn't make the connection immediately," Richard said. "But the first time I saw you, I thought you looked familiar. I realize now, it's because you look like Helen.

"It's not an obvious resemblance," he continued. "But your bone structure is the same, your eyes are the identical shape and color, even the way you move is similar."

"That's hardly conclusive," she scoffed.

He nodded. "There's something else Helen mentioned."

She swallowed, not wanting to ask the question and yet not able to hold it back. "What's that?"

"A birthmark."

Her hand went instinctively to her hip.

"The baby Helen gave up for adoption had a heart-shaped birthmark exactly where yours is."

She couldn't lie about the birthmark or deny its existence—he'd seen it, touched it, kissed it. Maybe that's why she felt so betrayed by these disclosures now. How could he do this to her? How could he even suggest something so ridiculous—especially when he knew she had no interest in her birth mother.

She stared at him through eyes blurred with tears, and asked, "Why are you doing this, Richard?"

"Because I think the only way you're going to overcome your doubts and insecurities is to face the past."

"*You* think? How could *you* know anything about my doubts and insecurities?" she challenged. "How could *you* understand what it's like to be unwanted? How could you possibly imagine what it's like to be discarded and forgotten?"

"You weren't unwanted or forgotten," he said softly.

"Maybe that's what *you* think—but the reality tells a different story."

"Why don't you meet Helen before you jump to any conclusions?" he suggested.

She shook her head, hating that he sounded so damn logical and reasonable when the jumble of emotions inside her was anything but. "I don't want to meet her."

He studied her for a long moment, and she somehow sensed that he was disappointed in her response.

"Okay," he said at last.

Okay?

She eyed him warily.

"It has to be your choice," he said. "And when you're ready, I know you'll make the right one. You just need some time to think about it."

She thought about it.

Throughout the afternoon, Jenny sat in front of her blank computer screen unable to do anything but think about what Richard had told her.

Could it possibly be true? Could Richard's boss be her birth mother? Jenny didn't think so. But why would Richard even suggest it if he didn't believe it could be true? As much as she wanted to continue to deny the possibility, her curiosity about Helen Hanson was piqued.

She did an Internet search, found a few articles, some more pictures. Usually Helen was with George Hanson, the media mogul, and gazing through adoring eyes at her much older husband. He was a handsome man, Jenny had to admit, but she wondered if the woman had been attracted by his looks as much as by his much more impressive wealth. Then he'd died, and Helen had found out the wealth wasn't quite what she'd expected it to be.

Maybe that was why she'd cooked up this story about an adopted child now. If Richard mentioned Jenny's name to his boss, it would have been easy enough for Helen to find out that she'd been adopted—and by a very wealthy family. With that information, she'd probably decided it would be easier to claim a long-lost daughter with a hefty trust account than to try and save her husband's failing business.

After the debacle of Brad's recent proposal, it was the scenario that made the most sense to Jenny. It certainly made more sense than believing it was a simple coincidence that her lover's boss could be her biological mother.

"Every time I'm here, you're clicking away on that computer—and you accused me of being a workaholic."

Jenny jolted at the interruption.

As if conjured by her thoughts, Brad was suddenly there.

"I thought you'd be back in New York by now," she said.

"It seemed a shame to come all this way and not take the time to see Tokyo. I spent the weekend sightseeing."

At least she didn't need to worry that she'd broken his heart when she turned down his proposal.

"I'm heading back tomorrow," he told her. "But I wanted to say goodbye before I left."

He glanced past her to the computer monitor. She inwardly cursed herself for not thinking to close the window when he'd shown up.

"What are you working on?" he asked.

"Just doing some research for a story on the TAKA merger with Hanson Media."

"Doesn't sound very interesting."

"It's not a natural disaster or civil war, so I guess it wouldn't seem too interesting to you," she agreed.

"Wow." Brad ignored her comment, his attention focused on the picture on the screen. "The Hanson widow looks remarkably like you."

Now she did click to close the window. "They say we all have a twin somewhere in the world," she said lightly.

His gaze narrowed on her. "Yeah," he agreed at last. "That's probably it."

She forced a smile. "Have a good trip back."

"Maybe I'll see you in New York sometime?"

"Maybe."

He hesitated a moment before bending to kiss her cheek, then he was gone.

She exhaled a shaky sigh of relief. Unfortunately, it wasn't so easy to get rid of the thoughts about Helen Hanson that plagued her mind.

She hadn't given Richard an answer about dinner with Helen. She wasn't sure what her answer would be. Her initial instinct had been to refuse—as if considering the invitation would give too much credence to the possibility that Helen was her birth mother. Then she resolved to accept, if only to prove that the claim was completely erroneous. Brad's reaction to Helen's picture made her rethink this position. What could meeting Richard's boss possibly prove except that there were some similarities in their appearance?

She was still undecided when she showed up at his suite later that afternoon. He'd given back the key card she'd returned last week, but she took a deep breath to steady her nerves and knocked.

* * *

Richard felt the strain in his smile when he opened the door and saw Jenny standing there. His brain scrambled for an out from what he already knew was an impossible situation as he heard himself say, "You're early."

Her smile was warm. "I couldn't wait to see you."

Normally the admission would have filled him with satisfaction. But there was nothing normal about the situation she was about to walk into, and he felt only trepidation as she stepped past him and into the room.

She halted abruptly, and he knew she'd spotted Helen standing on the other side of the room. She looked at him— shock, hurt and a hint of fear in her eyes.

Before he had a chance to say anything, Helen turned.

He heard her suck in a breath as her eyes locked on the younger woman. Her eyes widened and her face went pale, as if she was seeing a ghostly apparition—or the daughter she'd given up.

"Oh, my God."

Jenny was the first to look away, silently pleading for his help. But he didn't know what to do. As much as he'd wanted the two women to meet, he hadn't wanted it to happen like this.

"You promised that it would be my decision," she said. Her words were barely more than a whisper, but he heard the echo of her hurt, her distress, the belief he'd betrayed her.

"I didn't plan this, Jenny."

"Just another unlikely coincidence?" she asked, her tone laced with skepticism.

"It is," he insisted.

Helen had remained silent, listening to their exchange, but she finally spoke to Jenny. "You're my daughter."

Jenny shook her head. "My mother is Dana Anderson."

"She's your adoptive mother," Helen clarified.

"She's the only mother I have—the only one that matters."

Helen flinched as she absorbed the harsh words that were more a reprimand than a statement of fact. But it was the stark pain in Jenny's eyes that squeezed Richard's heart.

While revealing the truth seemed to him the obvious— and maybe the only—way to start to heal the wounds of the past for both of them, he hadn't wanted it to happen like this. Yes, Jenny needed to hear why Helen gave her up, to know that she wasn't unwanted. And Helen needed to know the woman her child had become, to understand that she'd made the right decision all those years ago. But he wished he hadn't found himself tangled up in the middle.

"I didn't mean to upset you," Helen said softly. "I'm just so glad to finally meet my daughter."

"I'm *not* your daughter," Jenny said. But the denial was shaky and her eyes were filled with tears when she turned toward the door.

"Jenny, wait—"

But she was already out the door.

She went to her parents' house. With her entire world crumbling around her, Jenny couldn't think of anywhere to go but home.

Dana was pulling weeds out of her flower beds when she arrived, but one look at her daughter's face and she peeled off her gardening gloves and went to her. "What's wrong?"

She couldn't answer. Her throat was tight, her eyes swimming with tears.

Her mother took her hand and led her over to the porch.

Jenny followed without protest, sitting down on the step beside her. It wasn't until her mother took her in her arms that Jenny let the tears fall. She couldn't hold them back any longer. Dana cuddled her as she had when she was a child, and Jenny cried as she hadn't cried since she was a child.

She cried until her eyes were swollen and her throat was raw, until she felt as if she didn't have any tears left inside.

Dana rubbed her hand over her back. "You're really starting to scare me, honey."

She lifted her head from the comfort of her mother's shoulder. "Sorry."

"I don't want you to be sorry, I want you to tell me what's wrong so I can help you."

"You've always been there for me," Jenny said. "Always, even when I didn't deserve it."

"You've always deserved it."

She managed a watery smile. "Even when I was a teenager, testing your patience?"

"Especially then." Dana kissed both of her daughter's tear-streaked cheeks. "No matter what, your dad and I will always love you."

Jenny blinked back fresh tears as she nodded, finally accepting it was true, acknowledging that the family she'd wanted so desperately had been there for her all along.

Richard checked her apartment and the newspaper, but couldn't find Jenny at either of those places. That left only one possibility that he could think of—her parents' home. While he wasn't anxious to face either Harold or Dana Anderson, his need to see Jenny left him with no other option.

Samara had given him the address, and Dana Anderson opened the door almost immediately after he pressed the bell.

"I need to see Jenny," he told her.

"She doesn't want to see you right now, Richard."

He wasn't surprised by the response, but he wouldn't let it deter him, either. "I'm not going anywhere until I talk to her."

Her lips curved ever so slightly. "I wonder if your stubbornness is any match for my daughter's."

"I'm not going to give up on her."

"You probably already know that Jenny doesn't do anything in half measures. When she loves, she loves completely. And when she hurts, she hurts deeply."

"I never wanted to hurt her."

"But that's what happened, isn't it?"

"I regret that Jenny met Helen the way she did," he said. "But I still believe she should know her birth mother."

"Because it's what your boss wants?" she challenged.

"Because it's what Jenny needs. I know you're her mother in every way that counts," he continued. "And Jenny knows that you love her, but she still has insecurities because of her adoption."

"You think knowing her birth mother will change that?"

"I think it's an important step."

"Even if it's not what she wants?"

He hesitated, then nodded.

"I happen to agree with you."

His surprise must have shown, because Dana smiled.

"Harold and I expected there would come a time when Jenny started asking questions about her adoption," she said. "But she never did. We knew she *had* questions—that was obvious in so many ways—but she never voiced them, at least not to us. I think she felt it would be disloyal to show any interest in her birth mother, or maybe she thought we would be hurt if she wanted to find her."

She sighed. "I saw how much she was hurting herself by keeping it all bottled up inside, and I tried to talk to her. Harold and I both did. But Jenny adamantly refused to discuss her birth mother and we never succeeded in forcing the issue."

"I don't think anyone forces Jenny to do anything."

"You do know my daughter."

"I love her, Mrs. Anderson."

Dana sighed again. "You're lucky Harold is in Singapore on business right now. He would have called the police and had you hauled off to jail for hurting his little girl."

"Am I safe in assuming you won't?"

"I won't," she agreed. "I also won't tell you that Jenny likes to sit by the pond out back when she needs to think."

Jenny was there, as her mother had said she would be.

Sitting alone on the grass, her chin resting on her bent knees, her arms wrapped around them. She looked like a child—lost and alone.

She didn't hear him approach, so Richard stood silent for several moments watching her, trying to find the words to repair the damage that he'd done. Her eyes were puffy and red-rimmed from crying, and he felt the sharp kick of guilt in his chest.

It didn't matter that he hadn't deliberately set up the meeting with Helen. What mattered was that he'd set everything in motion, and he was responsible for hurting her.

He sat down on the grass beside her.

She stiffened but gave no other indication that she was even aware of his presence.

They stayed that way, side by side and silent for several long minutes before he broke the silence. "How long do you think you can continue to ignore me?"

"Until you go away."

He shook his head. "You once accused me of being pushy. Well, I'm going to keep pushing until we deal with this."

"There's nothing to deal with."

He watched as a tear slid down her cheek, then another. "I love you, Jenny."

She shook her head fiercely. "Don't you dare say that to me now."

"It's true."

"If it was true, you wouldn't have ambushed me."

"I didn't invite Helen to my hotel suite. I wouldn't do that to you. But now that you've met her—"

"I didn't want to meet her." She stood up, finally turning to face him. "I thought I made it perfectly clear that I had no interest in finding my birth mother—and that applies to anyone claiming to be my birth mother, too."

He was silent for a moment before he said, "You should have heard her talking about the baby she'd given up—the grief in her voice."

"You should have heard *me* when I said I didn't want to know the woman who gave me away."

"I heard you," Richard admitted. "I just couldn't believe you really meant it. I can't believe you don't have questions."

"About the mother who abandoned me at birth?" she asked scornfully.

"About her *reasons* for giving you up."

"Well, I don't."

He still didn't believe her, but he knew it would serve

no purpose to press the issue now. "Then I'm sorry," he said, accepting that he did owe her an apology for the way events had unfolded, for causing her pain even if it had been inadvertent.

He reached for her, wanting to offer her comfort, wanting to draw her closer. She seemed so distant now— her hurt and anger a tangible barrier between them.

She pulled away from him.

"Please don't let this come between us."

"You put it between us," she said coolly. "When you put Helen's needs before mine."

"Dammit, Jenny. That's not how it happened."

"Isn't it?"

"No. I was only thinking about you."

But his words didn't sway her. He could tell she didn't believe him. In her entire life, no man had ever put her first. Certainly none of her ex-boyfriends had, and he couldn't blame her for being skeptical now.

"You need to talk to Helen," he said gently. "You need to hear from her why she made the decisions she did. Maybe then you'll finally stop feeling like you've always been second best."

She shook her head. "I'll stop feeling that way when other people stop treating me that way."

Then she turned and walked back to the house.

Jenny felt numb. The hurt and anger and confusion had all been washed away by the flood of tears, leaving her feeling only empty inside. Her emotions now spent, her mind started to sift through the bits of information she'd been given, forcing her to face new questions she wasn't sure she was ready to have answered.

Dana knocked softly on her door before entering the bedroom. The mattress dipped slightly as she sat beside her daughter. "I saw Richard leaving."

She didn't respond.

"Do you feel better knowing you hurt him, too?" The gentle tone failed to mask the censure in the question.

Jenny scowled. "I can't believe you're taking his side."

Her mother sighed. "It's not about taking sides, but I do think he wants what's best for you."

"Best would be not having Richard Warren make decisions for me."

"What about Helen Hanson?" Dana asked. "What are you going to do about her?"

She shrugged. "Nothing."

Dana waited.

"Despite her claims, I don't believe she's the woman who gave birth to me."

"Why not?"

"It's just too unbelievable that our paths would happen to cross the way they did. It's like something out of a bad movie."

"It does seem unlikely," Dana said.

Jenny wondered why her mother's agreement failed to appease her.

"And I don't need some stranger coming into my life at this stage and making such outrageous claims," she continued.

Dana nodded. "If her claim is truly outrageous."

She frowned. "Do you believe it could be true?"

"Are you asking that question because you really don't believe it—or because you don't want to know?"

Jenny wasn't sure how to respond.

"Because if you want the truth—" Dana placed an envelope on the bed "—you'll find it in there."

She stared at the label, noted that it was addressed to Harold and Dana Anderson, but didn't touch the package. "What is it?"

"It's the report of a private investigator your father and I hired to find your birth mother."

"When—why—" She shook her head, trying to organize the questions that were swirling around inside her head.

"About ten years ago," Dana said. "Because we thought there would come a time when you wanted to know. Because we thought you should know."

"Is it…Helen Hanson?"

"The investigator told us he found her and he'd send the report. But we never read it. It was for you, Jenny, not for us."

She picked up the envelope with trembling fingers, turned it over. She traced a fingertip over the seal, but made no move to open it.

"I don't think Richard would have even suggested the possibility that there was a connection between you and Helen if he wasn't absolutely certain," Dana said. "But you can stay mad at him and take comfort in not knowing for certain, or you can open the envelope."

Chapter Sixteen

Jenny took the envelope with her when she went back to her apartment. She put it on the dresser in her bedroom, where it seemed to mock her while she tried to sleep. Finally, at around three a.m. when she finally gave up the pretense, she climbed out of bed and carried it into the living room.

She turned on the small lamp beside the sofa and sat for several long minutes with it in her hand. She knew it wasn't going to stop nagging at her unless she either opened it or burned it. At the moment, she was in favor of fire—she wanted only to obliterate this evidence that had the power to turn her whole life upside down.

But she knew that wouldn't really change anything. It certainly wouldn't make the questions go away.

She slid a shaky finger under the flap, tearing the seal.

Her heart was pounding as she pulled the pages out of the envelope, her throat dry as she unfolded them.

She felt as if she was on a roller coaster, waiting for the big dip.

Re: Jennifer Anderson.

As her eyes scanned the black typeface on the paper, her heart settled into a familiar rhythm. There were no rises or heart-stopping falls, no quick bends or stomach-clenching turns. There was no shock or disbelief or even any anger left, because the words confirmed what she'd already known in her heart.

She folded the papers up, tucked them back into the envelope and fell asleep on the sofa.

Richard was on his way out the door when he spotted Helen striding briskly down the hall toward his room. Her face was paler than usual, her eyes dull—almost defeated.

He stepped back to let her inside, instinctively knowing that whatever had brought her to his room this morning when they both should have been on their way to TAKA was something they wouldn't want to talk about in the hall.

"Mori Taka is threatening to pull out of our deal."

She made the announcement without preamble when he'd closed the door behind her.

Richard frowned. "He can't do that."

"He can if there were material misrepresentations," she said.

"What are you talking about?"

She handed him a copy of the morning paper. He felt the beginning of a chill as he looked at the pictures of

Jenny and Helen side by side, a chill that grew colder upon scanning the headline. "Unexpected Family Reunion or Deliberate Corporate Plant?

The icy feeling spread as he read further.

> That is the question TAKA executives are pondering this morning in wake of the revelation that one of their own employees, American-born journalist Jenny Anderson, is the biological daughter of Hanson Media Group's CEO, Helen Hanson.
>
> Ms. Anderson came to Tokyo from New York City shortly after the death of Helen's husband, George Hanson, at about the same time it was discovered that the U.S. media giant was in extreme financial trouble.

Richard folded the paper. He didn't need to read any more to know that the article would hurt Jenny deeply and could be disastrous for the merger. As unhappy as she'd been to find out that Helen was her mother, he could only imagine how she'd feel having that information announced to the public—especially with the implication that she was working behind the scenes to help facilitate the merger with TAKA.

He wished he could be there for her, but Jenny had shut him out. She wouldn't even talk to him—never mind let him help her come to terms with the revelation. The only thing he could do now was focus his attention on the merger. It was the reason he'd come to Tokyo—and the only thing he had left.

Jenny dumped the paper into the recycle bin. She'd always been a private person and she felt sick at the thought of the intimate details of her personal life splashed across the newspaper for public consumption. And she was furious at the implication that she would let herself be used by anyone—even her biological mother—as an inside spy. Beneath the hurt and the anger, she was also determined. She might not be able to undo the damage that had been done, but she could track down the reporter and find the "anonymous inside source" who was responsible.

But aside from her parents and Helen, Samara and Richard were the only ones who knew the truth. She trusted her best friend implicitly and never entertained the possibility that she would leak such a hurtful story. She was just as convinced that Richard wasn't responsible for the headlines. Even though she was angry with him right now, she didn't believe for a minute he would do something like this. Besides, he had nothing to gain from the publicity and a whole lot to lose. If TAKA used the revelations as an excuse to pull out of the merger, the repercussions for Hanson Media Group would be a lot worse than her personal angst.

While Jenny didn't have any ready suspects, she was a reporter and she did have contacts in the newspaper world. The *Herald* had got the story from someone, and she was determined to uncover that source.

Helen returned to Chicago and tried to go about the day-to-day business of running a company whose future was increasingly uncertain. She could blame George for leaving Hanson Media in a hell of a mess, but she knew her own actions since taking the helm had only compounded the problems.

She'd been reluctant to leave Tokyo—for a lot of reasons, but especially because she didn't want to lose the daughter she'd just found. She'd tried contacting Jenny, by calling her apartment and visiting the newspaper. But Jenny refused to see her and in the end, she'd accepted that her presence was needed at home. Richard had remained in Japan to continue discussions with TAKA.

The phone on her desk buzzed and she sighed. Just one more interruption in a never-ending series of them.

"Yes?" she asked wearily.

"Jenny Anderson is here to see you."

The weariness was immediately replaced by equal parts anticipation and trepidation. The way things had played out the last time she'd seen her daughter—the first time since she'd given her up—she'd believed it might very well be the last time she saw her.

She didn't know what it meant that Jenny was here now, but she was anxious to find out. "Send her in."

Helen pushed her chair back and stood up, brushing her hands down the front of the navy skirt she wore, smoothing imaginary wrinkles. Her heart was pounding furiously and her chest was tight.

Then Jenny was there, standing in the doorway, and the love for her child that she'd kept bottled up inside for so long spilled over.

Don't rush, Helen reminded herself. Don't push for too much too soon. She'd made that mistake once already.

Jenny was here—she'd taken that first step. For now, that was enough.

"Hello, Jenny."

Her daughter hovered on the threshold between the corridor and Helen's office, hesitant, uncertain. "I probably should have made an appointment with your secretary to set up a more convenient time to see you."

"Of course not," she denied immediately. "Please, come in."

Jenny took two steps into the room, the distance of at least ten feet and twenty-five years still separating them.

"I didn't know you were planning a trip to Chicago."

"I wasn't." She took another tentative step forward. "It was my parents' idea."

Her parents being Harold and Dana Anderson, of course. Helen wondered if the choice of words was deliberate or not.

"They thought I should talk to you," she continued. "And I agreed."

Helen waited.

Jenny was clutching the strap of her purse so tightly her knuckles were white. Helen wanted nothing more than to comfort her child, ease her obvious pain. But she didn't delude herself into thinking this was a reunion—it was a confrontation. Her daughter's next words proved that.

"I'd like you to answer some questions. I would have asked them earlier, but you left Tokyo less than forty-eight hours after dropping the bomb that blew apart my life."

Helen looked away. "You wouldn't take my calls. I couldn't stay in Japan indefinitely, hoping you would talk to me."

"Why did you leave?"

"The news created a crisis for Hanson and since I was responsible, I needed to deal with the repercussions of it personally."

"What would you know about responsibility? It seems to me you're best at walking away from it."

It was a well-aimed blow and Helen took the hit, accepting there would be a lot more before she and Jenny came to any understanding of the past—if they ever did. "I can't blame you for thinking that, but you don't understand the circumstances that existed twenty-five years ago."

"You didn't want to be bothered with a child." She shrugged. "It doesn't seem all that complicated to me."

Helen's own hurt was forgotten as her heart broke open for the obvious pain hidden deep within her daughter's deliberately casual response. "If that's what you really believe, why are you here?"

She shrugged again. "I guess I just wanted to hear you admit it."

After too many years of wondering, Jenny wanted only to put the questions and doubts behind her. She'd spent too much time wondering about her birth mother, imagining various scenarios to explain why she'd been given away.

What she'd read in the private investigator's report gave her some answers but no explanations. Helen had been sixteen when she got pregnant, and although Jenny could muster some sympathy for a teenage girl with no education or resources to care for a baby, she didn't understand the twenty-five years of silence that had followed. In that time, Helen moved away from her controlling parents, went to college and married a wealthy and successful businessman—all without expressing any interest in the child she'd given up.

"I can't tell you that," Helen said softly. "Because the truth is that I wanted you more than anything else in the world."

Jenny refused to be swayed by the tears she saw shining in the other woman's eyes—eyes that she could admit now were almost exactly like her own.

"But I was still in high school and my family refused to support me if I kept my baby. I didn't want you growing up in that kind of home, anyway. I wanted you to have a loving home—a real family."

She remained silent.

"You're still skeptical," Helen said.

"I don't know what I expected you to say," she admitted. "And I guess there's a part of me that can't help thinking you've had twenty-five years to come up with a good story."

Helen opened the bottom drawer of her desk and pulled out a stack of envelopes. She pushed them across the desk toward Jenny. "You're right," she said. "I've had twenty-five years. And those are the letters I wrote on your birthday on each of the past twenty-five years. I want you to have them. Maybe then you'll understand that I spent every day of those twenty-five years wondering if I'd made a mistake. Questioning if there might have been some way I could have made it work. Hoping you were truly happy with the family you'd been given."

Jenny picked up the bundle of letters, noted that the envelope on top had the current year inscribed on it.

"I was happy," she said. "My parents are wonderful."

Helen nodded.

"You would have known that if you'd made any effort to find me."

"I'd relinquished my rights—along with my responsibilities—when I gave you up."

Jenny hesitated before asking, "If you really wished you could have kept me, why didn't you ever have any more children?"

"I wanted children," Helen told her. "More than anything, I wanted a baby to hold in my arms, to fill the emptiness in my heart that had been there since the day I gave you up. And we tried. George had three sons and I'd had you, so there didn't seem to be any reason we couldn't have a child of our own."

She looked away. "We tried everything, until I finally accepted that not being able to have another baby was my punishment for letting go of the one I'd been given."

Jenny felt the sting of tears in her own eyes. Regardless of what she wanted to believe, there was no denying the emotion she heard in Helen's voice.

She swallowed around the tightness in her throat. "It was Brad Morgan who leaked the story to the press."

Helen frowned. "The reporter?"

"And my ex-boyfriend," she admitted.

"Why did he do it?"

"To get back at me for rejecting him. I think he knew I decided not to marry him because of Richard, and it would have been a way to get back at him, too. But his primary motive was probably financial. I heard he was paid well for the exclusive."

"What is the situation with you and Richard?" Helen asked gently.

"There is no situation," she said.

"You're still angry with him, too," she guessed.

"No. Maybe." She sighed. "It doesn't really matter."

"Of course it matters."

Jenny shook her head.

"He loves you, Jenny. And you wouldn't still be hurting so much if you didn't love him, too."

She felt a sharp pang of regret, but accepted that the end of their relationship had always been inevitable.

"He called me yesterday," Helen continued.

Jenny didn't ask why. She told herself she didn't want

to know. It still hurt too much to think about everything they might have had.

"TAKA has agreed to resume negotiations," she explained, "and Richard needed my consent to put another condition on the table."

Helen paused, as if waiting for some kind of response, but she remained silent.

"He wants a position with Hanson in Tokyo when the merger goes through."

Jenny's gaze flew to Helen's; the other woman smiled.

"I told him it seemed like a reasonable request," she continued.

"Why?" Jenny asked softly.

"Obviously he wants to stay in Japan, and I can think of only one reason he would do that."

"He's starting to like sushi?" she asked weakly.

Helen laughed, then turned serious. "He loves you, Jenny, and he wants a chance to prove it."

Jenny tried to sort out her thoughts and feelings about Richard throughout the thirteen-hour flight back to Japan, but when the plane finally landed, she was still no closer to any answers. Despite Helen's assertion that Richard wanted to stay in Tokyo, she was afraid to let herself hope they could get past all the misunderstandings and build a future together.

She'd called her mother from the airport to let her know she was coming home. Dana had told her that she and Harold were going up to the cabin for a few days but would make arrangements for a car to pick Jenny up and drive her there. She was already looking forward to the peace and serenity of the lake, hoping the answers that eluded her might be found there.

It was almost nine p.m. when the car finally pulled into the narrow laneway that led to the cabin and Jenny was struggling to stay awake. Even though she'd only been gone a few days, her internal clock was having difficulty adjusting to the time difference, and she was looking forward to falling into bed and sleeping for twelve hours straight.

She didn't see him on the porch. She'd walked right past him, her hand reaching for the handle of the door, when the first notes of the music registered.

Her heart skipped a beat, then began thudding frantically against her ribs when she turned and saw Richard.

She swallowed, tried to speak, but her throat was tight. As the music played, memories of the night they'd sang this song together—the first night they'd made love—flooded over her, swamping her with emotion. It was the same night—though she wouldn't admit it until a long time later—she'd fallen in love.

Richard took a step toward her. "It's about time you got here."

She couldn't deny she was a little disappointed. She wasn't sure what she'd expected him to say, but after everything they'd been through, after coming home and finding him here, she'd expected…more.

"Have you been waiting long?" she asked, matching his casual tone.

He smiled as he took her hand in his, linked their fingers together. "I've been waiting for you forever."

And with those words, her heart simply melted. It wasn't just the incredibly romantic words, it was the sincerity in his voice and the love shining in his eyes. It was the "more" she'd been hoping for, and then some.

"I love you, Jenny."

Her throat was tight again, but she managed to respond. "I love you, too."

"Enough to marry me?" he asked. Then, with his free hand, he pulled a box out of his pocket and flipped open the lid.

She gasped softly and took an instinctive step back.

"That's not quite the reaction I was hoping for," Richard said.

Her gaze darted from his face to the gold band sparkling with diamonds, and back again, while the music continued to play in the background. "You can't mean it."

"Why can't I?"

"Because you don't want to get married."

"I've got a ring right here that says otherwise," he told her.

"You don't have to do this, Richard."

"I *want* to."

She swallowed. "Why?"

"Because I love you, and I'm hoping you'll overlook all the things I've done to screw up our relationship and marry me anyway."

This time her heart did sing with joy, but she forced herself to show some restraint. She didn't want him to feel pressured or coerced in any way. She needed to know that he wanted this as much as she did.

"We both screwed up," she said softly.

"Yeah, but that doesn't make a very romantic sounding proposal."

She smiled. "You have a point."

"And you still haven't answered my question."

"I don't remember actually hearing a question."

His gaze was unwavering, the love he felt shining clearly in his eyes. "Will you marry me, Jenny?"

She exhaled an unsteady breath.

"You better mean it," she warned him. "Because if I put that ring on, I'm not ever taking it off."

He reached for her hand and slid the circle of diamonds onto her finger.

It fit perfectly.

Jenny didn't know what time it was when Richard shook her awake, she only knew that when she opened her eyes it was still dark and, therefore, obviously not morning. She closed her eyes again.

"If you don't get up, you're going to miss the sunrise," he warned.

"It'll happen again tomorrow," she reminded him.

"I want to see it today," he said. "And if you don't get up and get dressed, I'll carry you outside naked."

She didn't doubt it. After last night, she wasn't sure there was anything he wouldn't do. She pushed herself up and tried to stifle a yawn. "I thought you weren't a morning person."

He smiled. "I wasn't—until I had the life-altering experience of making love with you as the sun rose."

"Life-altering?" she said skeptically, tugging on the clothes that had been hastily shed beside the bed the night before.

"Absolutely." He brushed his lips over hers. "Come on, I've got coffee on."

She stifled another yawn as she followed him down the hall. She took her cup of coffee outside, cradling it in her hands as she snuggled against Richard's chest. Despite her teasing, she understood what he meant about life-altering experiences, and she knew that meeting him had been such an experience for her.

He'd helped her to face her past and inspired her to look forward to their future. He'd shown her what it was to truly love and be loved. He'd done so much for her, she'd wanted to do something for him in return. It had seemed like a good idea at the time, but now she wasn't sure if he'd appreciate her effort or think she'd overstepped her bounds.

In either case, she wasn't going to embark on a future with any secrets between them.

"There's something I meant to tell you last night—before we got distracted."

"What is it?"

"When I went to the States, I didn't just go to Chicago."

"Where'd you go?"

"Crooked Oak, North Carolina."

She felt the tension in the arm that was wrapped around her, although his voice was neutral when he spoke. "I didn't know you knew anyone there."

"I didn't," she admitted. "Not until I met your mother."

He didn't say anything.

"I thought, since it was a trip about mending fences, that I would make the effort."

He sighed. "I appreciate what you were trying to do, Jenny, but you don't know my family."

"She misses you, Richard. She knows she was wrong to say the things she said, to make the demands she made. She just doesn't know how to bridge the gap she's created between you—or even if you want her to." She turned to face him. "She didn't even know you were in Japan."

He shrugged, but she saw the flicker of guilt in his eyes. "I haven't talked to her in a while."

"You should call her."

He hesitated briefly, then nodded.

"Will you?" she asked, pressing for verbal confirmation.

"I'll call her," he agreed.

She smiled and leaned forward to press a brief kiss to his lips. "Thank you."

"I should probably be thanking you," he said. "But I'm not convinced this is going to work."

"It will," she said confidently. "If I can overcome the barriers of twenty-five years to patch things up with Helen, you can reconcile with your mother."

"This really matters to you, doesn't it?"

She nodded. "Because you reminded me how important family is, and I know how much yours means to you." She smiled. "And because I want a big traditional wedding and they're your family."

"Except that you couldn't have known I was going to propose when you went to see my mother."

She shrugged. "Maybe I figured I owed you some interference after you made me confront my past."

"You can spend the rest of your life interfering in mine," he told her.

"I will," she said. "Forever."

Gold and crimson light spilled into the sky as their lips met—the signal of a new day and the promise of a new life together.

* * * * *

*Don't miss the exciting conclusion
of the new Special Edition continuity,*
THE FAMILY BUSINESS
*From reader favorite
Allison Leigh*
MERGERS & MATRIMONY
*When Helen Hanson set out to prove her worth to her
troublesome stepsons, she knew it would be a risky
venture. But when she found herself falling hard for her
business rival, Mori Taka, her life as she knew it
changed—for the better!*
On sale June 2006, wherever Silhouette Books are sold.

**Hidden in the secrets of antiquity,
lies the unimagined truth...**

Introducing

ROGUE
ANGEL™

a brand-new line filled with mystery
and suspense, action and adventure,
and a fascinating look into history.

And it all begins with DESTINY.

In a sealed crypt in
France, where the
terrifying legend of
the beast of Gevaudan
begins to unravel,
Annja Creed discovers
a stunning artifact
that will seal her destiny.

*Available every other
month starting
July 2006, wherever
you buy books.*

**GOLD
EAGLE** ®

GRA1

HOTEL MARCHAND

**Four sisters.
A family legacy.
And someone is out to destroy it.**

**A captivating new limited
continuity, launching June 2006**

The most beautiful hotel in New Orleans,
and someone is out to destroy it. But mystery,
danger and some surprising family revelations
and discoveries won't stop the Marchand sisters
from protecting their birthright...
and finding love along the way.

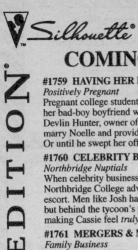

COMING NEXT MONTH